D0419283

DOMINICK ABEL LITERARY AGENCY, INC.
146 West 82nd Street, Suite 1B
New York, New York 10024
(212) 877-0710

Too Many Tomcats and Other Feline Tales of Suspense

Too Many Tomcats and Other Feline Tales of Suspense

Barbara Collins

edited and introduced by
Max Allan Collins

Five Star
Unity, Maine

Additional copyright information on page 211.

This bookl is a work of fiction. Names, characters, places, and incidents are either the product of the author's imagination, or, if real, used fictitiously.

Five Star First Edition Mystery Series.

Published in 2000 in conjunction with Tekno Books and Ed Gorman

The text of this edition is unabridged.

Set in 11 pt. Plantin by Elena Picard.

Printed in the United States on permanent paper.

Library of Congress Cataloging-in-Publication Data

Collins, Barbara, 1948–
  Too many tomcats and other feline tales of suspense / Barbara Collins ; edited and introduced by Max Allan Collins.
    p. cm.—(Five Star first edition mystery series)
    Contents: A proper burial—The ten lives of Talbert— To kill a cat—That damn cat—Obeah, my love—The night it rained cats and cats—Aunt Emma's defense—Cat got your tongue—Carry's cat—To Grandmother's house we go —Too many tomcats.
  ISBN 0-7862-2899-7 (hc : alk. paper)
  1. Detective and mystery stories, American. 2. Cats— Fiction. I. Collins, Max Allan. II. Title. III. Series.
PS3553.O474777 T66 2000
813′.54—dc21   00-061726

For Sharen —
my cat-loving friend

Table of Contents

An Introduction
by Max Allan Collins

It's my privilege to edit the first collection of a short story writer I greatly admire—and envy.

My wife, Barbara Collins, came to writing through the backdoor. For many years, she used her native intelligence and instinctive story sense to edit my novels and occasional short stories. In the late '70s, when I was writing the *Dick Tracy* comic strip, she began to assist me, writing the famous "Crimestopper's Textbook" feature. Later, she took over the *Mike Mist* "minute mystery" feature in the back of *Ms. Tree*, the comic book written by me (and drawn by Terry Beatty), to lighten my workload—and because I had run dry on ideas for two-page mystery stories.

She was surprisingly adept at it, for someone who had never aspired to writing, and later—when Terry Beatty's schedule also became overloaded—she began writing the *Mike Mist* feature in prose form. These early short stories of Barb's blew me away—they were so good I remember thinking, "She's a little *too* good." I had labored at my craft since junior high school, and here Barb had absorbed just about everything I know about writing, just by editing me—through sheer osmosis.

In 1990, when the *Dick Tracy* movie led to a number of licensing opportunities, including my first movie novelization, I invited Barb to write a story about Dick Tracy's wife, Tess

7

Trueheart, for the collection Dick Tracy: The Secret Files, edited by myself and anthology king, Marty Greenburg. Barb's story was one of the best in the book, impressing not only her husband but his co-editor: Marty began inviting Barb into anthologies of original stories.

While Barb contributed to any number of such thematic books edited by Marty, Ed Gorman and/or myself, among others, earning glowing reviews and berths in several "best of" collections and on "notable stories" lists—she received perhaps the most attention for the stories she wrote about cats, often for the bestselling *Cat Crimes* series. On the one hand, this is to be expected, because cat-loving mystery fans are legion; but on the other hand, it's flat out weird, because Barb is not only *not* a cat lover (we have always had dogs), she is allergic to the damn things.

So, frequently in a Barbara Collins story, the cat is either evil or dead or the victim of some crime or criminal scheme or other. It was rather a surprise, when I began looking through Barb's tales, with an eye on putting together her first collection, that she had written so many stories about the little furry creatures.

Not all of the stories herein originally appeared in the *Cat Crimes* anthologies. For example, one of them ("Obeah, My Love")—which won Barb incredible notices—was originally published in an erotic noir anthology; two are original stories, one written especially for this volume ("The Night It Rained Cats and Cats") and the other ("Aunt Emma's Defense") intended for a *Cat Crimes Goes to Court* anthology, but never submitted, as the deadline came and went before the story had received its final polish.

This is not surprising, because Barb is not a fast writer. She is a good writer, sometimes a wonderful one—but not fast. Like the classic short-story writer she is, she hones, polishes, focuses in, crafting her miniatures with a watchmaker's care.

I am a pretty damn good short story writer myself (and even co-wrote one of the stories in this book, "Cat Got Your Tongue"); and I am proud to have served in the same editorial capacity on these stories that Barb, over the many years of our marriage, has on my novels. Anything you read of hers has a little of me in it; and anything you read of mine has at least a little of her in it.

But Barb is, as I have often said, the best short story writer in this family.

I love her anyway.

—Max Allan Collins

A Proper Burial

Officer John Steele didn't want to do it.

He didn't want to tell Ernie and Marie Finley that the police had found their Sarah—who'd been missing for several days—dead.

As Steele stood on the doorstep of the Finley's modest, white stucco house, he hesitated to ring the doorbell. It wasn't as if he'd never been the bearer of bad news; like the time he told the Johnsons their son had been found—just so many body parts—in the woods of Wild Cat Den State Park. And then there was the Penmark girl who was raped, doused with gasoline and set on fire . . .

But somehow, this one was harder for Steele. His fellow officers on the force would be surprised if they knew just how much John was upset by the death of little Sarah. Because what they didn't know about John—whose cold, harsh manner made children quiver and criminals cower—was, that behind those piercing Clint Eastwood eyes, and inside that six-foot-three body-by-Hulk, lived a pussycat.

Suddenly the front door opened. Mr. Finley, who had either seen, or sensed, Officer Steele out on the porch, stood in the doorway. He was a small man, about five foot five, with a mustache, thinning brown hair, and a kind face etched with worry.

"You have news about Sarah?" he asked anxiously.

Officer Steele didn't answer immediately. He stepped inside, removing his hat, turning it slowly in his hands. For a

11

brief second or two he took in the surroundings, which surprised him.

Everything in the very formal living room was purple.

And now, something made sense: earlier he had trouble finding the Finleys, who'd just moved into the neighborhood. When he stopped some kids down the block to inquire about the family, one older boy had said, "You mean the purple people?"

Mrs. Finley joined them, having come out of the kitchen, wiping her hands on a lavender dish cloth. She was a few inches taller than her husband, and a few pounds heavier. Her jet black hair, piled on top of her head in huge, looping curls as if wrapped around soup cans, appeared to have a deep purple sheen under the light on the ceiling.

Officer Steele opened his mouth, but before he could speak, Mrs. Finley burst into tears, burying her face into the towel, as if she knew what he was about to say.

"I'm sorry," Steele said, his voice cracking as he fought to get himself under control. "Your Sarah's been killed."

Mr. Finley threw his arms around his wife, and they stood sobbing, so close together, the two became one.

"She was struck by a truck," Steele continued, "in front of a convenience store about a half a mile from here."

The Finleys sobbed harder.

Officer Steele, feeling awkward, touched the arm of the husband, whose face was burrowed into his wife's shoulder. Steele said quietly, "It was dark outside when she crossed the street, probably attracted by the lights . . . a woman—an off-duty nurse—saw what happened and ran to Sarah, but it was too late. The nurse eased her over to the curb and called us. The driver of the vehicle never stopped."

Mrs. Finley pulled away from her husband. The tears streaming down her face left tracks of purple mascara. "It's all my fault!" she wailed. "I left her in the kitchen to go up-stairs . . . and she must have gone out on her own, and gotten lost . . ." She looked toward the heavens—in this case, the ceiling—and screamed, "Oh, my baby! My baby!"

Mr. Finley grabbed his wife by her arms, almost shaking her, pleading. "It's *not* your fault! You *mustn't* blame your-self."

Officer Steele shifted his weight uneasily and cleared his throat. "Mr. and Mrs. Finley. I need you to come with me. To identify her."

Mrs. Finley's hand flew to her face as she gasped in horror at the thought of it, but Mr. Finley looked directly at the of-ficer. "We're ready," he said firmly. "Where do we go?"

"Downtown. The Forensic Lab," said Officer Steele softly.

"The Forensic Lab?" Mr. Finley asked, raising his eye-brows.

"Yes," said Officer Steele, putting on his hat, "we're gath-ering evidence so we can nail the killer who ran your little Sarah down."

Walter Graves was the best forensic expert in the state—hell, the whole *country*—but he'd be damned if he could figure a way to get the evidence the D.A. wanted for *this* case.

He unzipped the small body bag that lay on the shiny chrome table, then stroked his close-cut, grey beard as he stared at the bag's contents. Coming in the wake of his bril-liance in the Fernando trial—which brought his nation-wide—hell, *worldwide*—publicity, this one could only make him look like a fool!

He picked up the bag with both arms and carried it to a locker nearby, within which he carefully placed it before shutting the drawer. Yes, this one was important. Not because a life was lost—but because the eyes of the forensic field were upon him. Watching. Waiting . . . for him to step on his dick.

The door to the lab opened and a police officer Graves recognized—but did not know by name—entered, along with a middle-aged man and woman; he looked like Mr. Whipple from the old toilet paper commercials—she had weird hair.

"Mr. Graves," said the cop, gesturing to the couple, "this is Mr. and Mrs. Finley."

"Yes?" Graves said, keeping the irritation of this interruption out of his voice.

"They're here to identify . . . Sarah."

"Sarah?"

"Didn't someone from the desk call?"

"Oh, *Sarah*," Graves said, nodding. "Yes. But I don't know *what* they expect to be able to identify."

The missus began to cry and the husband tried to comfort her. Graves thought the cop shot him a dirty look.

"She's over here in cold storage," Graves said, moving to the wall of lockers.

The husband started forward, but the wife, shaking, held back. The cop put a massive arm around her shoulders, and with the help of the husband, they all moved forward.

Graves pulled open the drawer.

The trio advanced and stared.

"If it makes you feel any better," Graves said, trying to be helpful to the obviously distressed couple, "she didn't suffer—well, suffer *much*. I mean, she *did* get hit by a two-ton truck."

The little woman wailed, and the cop glared.

Graves, unable to make his voice sound pleasant any longer, said, "Well, is that her?"

"Yes," answered the husband, softly.

The wife nodded, unable to speak, wiping her eyes with a hankie.

"Reminds me of old Cornwall, back on the farm," sniffed the cop. "Got caught in a combine."

"Can we take her now?" said the missus, reaching for the body.

Graves lunged forward, covering the plastic bag, protectively, with both hands. "No!"

The wife's face turned angry. "No? *Why not?* She's *ours!*"

"She's state's evidence, now," Graves said flatly, withdrawing his arms from over the flattened form.

"For what?" asked the husband.

"For a murder investigation."

The cop intervened. "Mr. and Mrs. Finley, just moments before Sarah was run down, the manager of the convenience store was robbed and killed. A woman—the nurse who went to Sarah's aid—saw a man leave in a truck. While the nurse was able to give a good description of the man, the prosecutor needs corroborating evidence to make his case."

"But I don't understand what that has to do with Sarah, and why we can't take her!" said the wife.

"Because *Sarah* is the prosecutor's key piece of evidence!" Graves almost shouted at the woman. "I'll make this as simple as I can . . ." Graves continued, "Do you see those tire tracks?" He pointed to places on the remains. "They can identify the vehicle and in turn, the killer. Consequently, I can't release her until the suspect goes to trial."

"So you're talking . . ." said Mr. Finley, clearly ahead of his wife.

"A year. Maybe more."

The missus turned to her husband, her eyes pleading. He shook his head. She then faced the cop. "Officer Steele, please, make him give us Sarah! I can't bear to think of her lying in a *freezer* . . ."

The cop looked down at her. "You want the murderer convicted, don't you?"

"I suppose so," she said, half-heartedly. "But it's just not fair! First our Sarah is killed, and now, we can't even give her a proper burial."

Graves had had it.

"Jesus, lady!" he said, "It's just a goddamn *cat!*"

The cop gave Graves one last look that could kill, before walking the grieving couple gingerly out.

Marie Finley couldn't eat, could only sleep fitfully, since the death of Sarah. Under different circumstances, she would have been thrilled to lose the ten pounds that had melted away like butter; but she barely noticed, staying in her bathrobe most of the time. Her hair, normally so carefully done up in the same style as when she and Ernie first met, hung straight, limp, matted to her head. She sat in their bedroom, in a chair in the corner, caught in the grasp of depression, which was squeezing, and squeezing.

"Honey, please," said Ernie softly, entering the room with a tray of food. "You have to eat."

She didn't look at him.

"Sarah would want you to."

"How do you know what Sarah would want?!" Marie snapped viciously. "Sarah is *dead!*"

Ernie's face looked as if it had been slapped, and she was sorry she said it, but didn't take it back.

Ernie set the tray down on the bed, and turned to leave. "She had a good life," he said in a lame attempt to cheer her.

She didn't respond.

"I'm going to run an errand," he sighed. "I'll be back soon."

Marie watched him leave. Poor Ernie, she thought, poor, sweet Ernie. She knew he was hurting. But she couldn't help him. Not now. How could she, when she couldn't help herself. No, he would have to be the strong one. He always was.

They'd met at a concert almost nine years ago. It was during the summer of '83. "The Golden Boys of Bandstand," featuring Bobby Rydell, Frankie Avalon and Fabian, had played to a sold-out crowd of middle-aged bobby-soxers trying to relive *their* golden years. Afterwards, backstage, Marie managed to get Fabian to autograph her "Like a Tiger" 45 picture sleeve she'd brought along, and when he did, he looked at her and grinned, "Darlin', I *love* your hair." She thought she would *die!* She turned to the man next to her—another autograph seeker—and said, "He's still *so* cute!" When the crowd began to leave, the man—Ernie—and she walked back to the parking lot, talking excitedly about the performers—Ernie had every record Bobby Rydell ever made—and ended up going out for a malt. It was just like high school, but better!

She and Ernie were married a year later, a first time for both. But living together was hard, after being alone for so long. And when the children they wanted didn't arrive, Marie became depressed, and the marriage faltered. Ernie had read somewhere that the color purple was supposed to spark passion, and set about re-decorating their house. When that didn't work, he went away.

It was a cold, overcast day in November, several months later, when Ernie came back to Marie, begging her to give the marriage one last try. He was holding a package—a brightly wrapped box—and when she opened it, she saw a cute, cuddly, furry yellow cat with the most adorable blue eyes!

And they called her Sarah.

Marie got up from her chair in the bedroom. Like a phantom she floated down the hall, as if drawn by some invisible force, until she stood in front of a closed bedroom door. She knew if she opened it and went in, she'd break down. But she couldn't stop the hand that reached out and turned the knob, no more than she could stop the ache in her heart.

The late summer sun shone through a window and across a small bed—Sarah's bed. Marie felt the tears beginning to flow.

It was Christmastime, and she and Ernie were out shopping when they saw the doll bed—along with a little dresser and nightstand—in the window of Ingram's Department store. They bought the whole set for Sarah, laughing and giggling all the way home . . .

Marie could bear to look no longer, and turned to leave, shutting the door behind her; the room would remain untouched until Sarah was brought home to rest under the magnolia tree, in the back yard.

Ernie came in the kitchen door as Marie shuffled in, returning the untouched tray. He walked over to her, cupping her face in his hands.

"Marie," he said, "I went to see Officer Steele."

Marie looked right through him.

"The man that killed Sarah is out on bail."

She continued to stare.

"I found out where he lives."

Now his face came into focus.

"I know how we can get Sarah back," Ernie said, then smiled.

And for the first time in weeks, Marie felt blood in her veins.

And saw life in Ernie's eyes.

★ ★ ★ ★ ★

Virgil Wykert sat on his davenport and belched—loudly, rudely. He loved to do that, and was sorry no one was around to hear it. No one, that is, except for Dave, his pit bull. Dave lifted his huge head off the floor, where he'd been sleeping, stuck out his tongue, panted and drooled. Virgil's friends said the dog stunk, but *he* never noticed. Virgil leaned back and took another swig of beer, then reached down and scratched at his crotch. He'd better do something about those fleas, though, or the mutt would have to find his *own* bed to sleep in.

It was well after midnight but Virgil was up, playing with his new toy, a Turbo Graphx 16, one of the perks from the convenience store robbery. He'd gone out and bought it the very next day. The system was so much *better* than Nintendo. And the graphics of the games were sharper—like in the one he was playing—SPLATTERHOUSE; when the guts began to splatter, it looked so real! But the ghouls were getting the better of Virgil, partly because he was tired but mostly because he was drunk. He used the control pad to decapitate one of the monsters, and watched the blood ooze . . .

He hadn't planned on killing that store manager. But when the guy started whining about how he had a wife and a baby and all, something snapped inside Virgil. He just wanted him to *shut up!* Hell, *everybody* had it tough these days!

Virgil paused the video game, freezing its gory image on the television screen. He'd have to ice that eye witness, too—that nurse who fingered him . . .

There was a knock at the front door.

Virgil jumped, like the control with its wires had shocked him; he reached for the .38 hidden under the cushion, in case it was the cops, or some vengeance-seeking relative of that store manager.

"Yeah?" he hollered from the couch.

The knocking persisted.

Virgil got up and went to the door, holding the .38 hidden with his right hand, while cracking the door with his left.

"Whadaya want," he growled to the small, wimpy looking man on his stoop.

"Mr. Wykert?"

"I don't need any of what you're sellin'," Virgil snarled.

"Oh," the man said, "I'm not *selling* anything."

"Then *what?*" Virgil opened the door wider, flashed the gun and smiled smugly as the little man's eyes popped. Dave, now next to his master, growled viciously.

"I . . . I just wanted to talk to you about my cat . . ." the guy stammered, looking down nervously at the dog.

"Cat?" Virgil's eyes narrowed.

"Yes. The one you ran over in front of the convenience store you robbed."

Virgil reached out and grabbed the man by his coat collar, pulling him roughly to him, sticking the .38 under his chin. "I don't know what you're talkin' about. And if you don't want to be my dog's next meal, you'd better *leave!*"

Virgil gave him a shove, then reached out and grabbed him again. "No, *wait!*" he said, having a thought, "time is money. An' you just *wasted* my time—so give me some *money!*"

Still held in Virgil's grasp, the man got out his wallet, hands shaking. "Fifty's all I got."

Virgil grabbed the wallet and took out the money, then tossed it back and started to shut the door. "Oh, and by the way, *pop,*" he smirked, "I could have *missed* that kitty, but I *didn't.* Because, know what? *I hate cats!*"

Virgil slammed the door in the guy's startled face, and threw the lock.

He returned to the couch, laughing, thumbing the money

in his fingers. Now he could get the *other* Turbo Graphx game he wanted—LEGENDARY AXE!

But his laughing stopped abruptly, at a noise he heard outside: the unmistakable sound of the engine of his Chevy truck.

Virgil dropped the cash, picked up the .38 and ran out the door, with Dave right on his heels.

It was dark outside, but a three-quarter moon hung high in the sky, throwing a small spot-light on his most prized possession, which sat on the crest of his driveway, about five hundred feet from the house. The truck faced him, its headlights cutting through the air like laser swords in a video game. The teeth of the custom-made chrome grill, glinting in the moonlight, made an awesome mouth. The engine went BA-ROOM! BA-ROOM!

Virgil, face red with rage, started up the incline, gun in hand, snarling dog at his feet.

"Get outta my *truck,* you *son of a bitch!*" he hollered above the noise of the engine.

But as he approached, the truck slowly moved backwards, keeping its distance. He broke into a run now, pointing the gun, wanting to blast the bastard away, but he *couldn't* because he didn't want to hit his truck!

Suddenly big wheels squealed, and the Chevy jumped forward.

Dave took off for the hills, but Virgil froze in his tracks as the truck lunged toward him. He turned and started to run, but the teeth snatched him. And the mouth chewed him. And the truck devoured him, before coming to a stop, belching up smoke and blood . . .

The first purple-pink rays of the sun appeared on the horizon as Ernie opened the back door to the kitchen for his wife. They had driven around aimlessly, silently, for a long time, caught in those late hours between darkest despair and the dawning of hope.

"Ernie," Marie asked, breaking their self-imposed silence, "where on earth did you learn to hot-wire a car?"

Ernie removed his jacket, hanging it on a coat rack by the door. He turned to look at her, smiling shyly. "I used to work on jalopies when I was in high school. Trying to get the girls to like me."

She went to him, and looked at him the way a man always wanted a woman to. "*I* like you," she whispered, putting her hands on his shoulders. She kissed him; and the kiss that began soft and sweet, turned hot with love—and passion.

"Are you hungry?" she asked when their lips parted.

"Starving," he said.

"Me too! I'll make us some breakfast."

Ernie sat down at the round oak table, and Marie busied herself at the stove, and before too long she placed a big plate of scrambled eggs, bacon and hash browns in front of him.

"Oh, Ernie," she said, excitedly, joining him at the table, "that was such a *great* plan. Without a suspect, there'll be no trial, and they'll give us Sarah back." Her eyes were large and bright; then suddenly they clouded. "But I was so worried about you, when you went to his door."

Ernie stopped eating, fork in mid-air. "I had to make sure it was him."

"I know, but when he grabbed you and I saw a *gun*, I didn't know . . ."

Ernie sat up straight in his chair, looking toward the kitchen door.

Marie's eyes followed his. "What?" she asked quietly.

"Did you hear something? Outside?" Ernie asked, putting his fork down on his plate. "There. That."

22

Marie looked frightened. "Ernie," she whispered, "what if we were followed?"

"Couldn't have been," he said, then patted her hand, which was resting on the table. "It's nothing. We're just . . . jumpy."

He pushed his chair back, motioning Marie to stay put, went over to the door, and cautiously opened it.

Ernie looked out and didn't see anyone, but Marie let out a blood-curdling scream.

Ernie spun around, his heart pounding. He thought she had screamed in terror, until he saw the joy on her face and the yellow fur in her arms.

"Sarah!" Marie cried from down on the floor where she now sat with the cat held tightly to her chest. "It's *Sarah!*"

Ernie stared in disbelief, then ran to them, and fell on his knees, "Oh, my God . . . oh, my God . . . it *is* her!"

"You bad, bad cat!" Marie scolded between sobs. "*Where* have you *been?* Don't you know how *upset* we were?"

The cat, struggling to get free, jumped out of Marie's hands and ran to its dish that lay empty by the door.

"Ernie!" Marie shouted, "she's hungry! Quick, get the food!"

Ernie dashed to the cupboard and got out a can, and emptied it in the dish. And they watched the cat eat, tears of happiness running down their cheeks.

Then Marie picked up the cat. "Mama's baby must be *so* tired," she said, kissing its diffident face. "We're *all* tired. Let's go to bed."

"Good idea," Ernie yawned, turning out the kitchen light, following his wife out of the kitchen. "What a night!"

But at the bottom of the stairs, Marie, cat cradled in her arms, stopped in her tracks. "Oh, Ernie," she said, horrified, "what about that *man* . . . ?"

Ernie's face turned to stone. "He got what he deserved."

Marie nodded slowly, scratching the top of the cat's head. "That's right. After all, he was a *murderer*." She turned and climbed the stairs, nuzzling the cat, cooing quietly to it.

"I should say," Ernie said, following her up. "He killed a cat."

The Ten Lives of Talbert

At eight a.m. on Rodeo Drive, the immaculate street was devoid of its native Jaguars, Rolls-Royces and Ferraris. The only vehicles, prowling or parked, were of the dreary domestic variety—Ford, Chevrolet, Dodge—but for the occasional Japanese, which were only a marginal step up.

The sidewalks, too, were deserted, except for a few shoppers hovering near the fashionable storefronts, waiting for the doors to open.

Tourists.

Charles watched them from inside the locked glass door of his exclusive boutique, Chez Charles. He could tell they were tourists, no matter how well they dressed, because the real people of Beverly Hills simply never came out until the sun burned the haze out of the air.

He hated them. The *touriste*. Clopping into his shop in their *vulgaire* shoes and *pret-a-porter* clothing, carrying bourgeois bags, smelling of cheap eau de toilette . . . Why, they couldn't even afford a simple bauble, let alone a creation from his chic spring *haute couture!*

So when the *racaille*—the riff-raff—came in, he would raise his eyebrows in surprise and look down his nose at them disdainfully and say, *"Oui?"*, drawing the word out as if it were three. That was enough to make most flee.

But every once in a while some stupid woman would pretend she was actually interested in purchasing a ten-thousand-dollar, hand-beaded gown. When that happened Charles would gaze at her appraisingly, then state condescendingly that his creations did not come in *grande* sizes.

Charles made a disgusted sound with his lips as he stood waiting by the front glass door; just the thought of some . . . *paysan* . . . trying on one of his magnificent gowns made his skin crawl. His designs were only for the rich and famous!

A sleek white limousine pulled up.

Instantly excited, Charles unlocked the door with a trembling hand and stepped out into the pleasant spring morning.

Even now, he couldn't believe his luck! When the call had come in a month ago, he thought it a hoax: a woman claiming to be the great Simone Vedette, enduring icon of the '30s silver screen. He nearly slammed the phone receiver down. Because, except for some fleeting tabloid snap-shots taken of the actress on a beach somewhere, and a trashy unauthorized biography written by the woman's adopted daughter, the reclusive star had avoided contact with the public for over forty years!

But as Charles listened to the woman's low, sensual voice, laced with aristocratic breeding, the more he believed the call was authentic.

She told him she was being honored at the Academy Awards, and had, after much coaxing, agreed to personally accept the Oscar for Lifetime Achievement. She needed a gown—a beautiful dress—like the ones she had recently spotted in his store window. Could she see him some morning before hours?

And now, the aged immortal star—really the only legend left alive since the deaths of Dietrich and Garbo—was about to exit the limo, its windows darkened for privacy, to purchase a gown from him! From Chez Charles! Elusive fame would at last be his. Once he leaked the news to the tabloids, that is.

The chauffeur, a middle-aged man with greying temples, smartly dressed in uniform and cap, opened the car's back door.

Charles wiped his sweating palms on the sides of his tailored trousers. Moved closer to the curb.

But instead of the living legend, out of the back of the limo climbed a plain-faced woman of Mexican descent who could have been thirty, or forty or fifty years old, wearing a cotton print house-dress, horned-rimmed glasses and oversized head-scarf.

This was not Simone Vedette!

Perhaps under different circumstances, Charles would have laughed at the ludicrousness of such a common woman getting out of limousine; but instead he stood frozen in disappointment and confusion.

But then the peasant woman turned and bent slightly and extended a hand into the car.

A long, slender gold-braceleted arm appeared, taking that hand, then a shapely black-nyloned leg extended outward toward the curb, as the great Simone Vedette was helped from the limo.

Charles sighed with relief, then grinned with pleasure. The Grande Dame of the Cinema was still quite beautiful!

She was small, perhaps five foot three, not the five foot seven or eight he had imagined. She wore a simple, black dress (too short) and a large, wide-brimmed black hat (too big). A gold necklace (too heavy) graced her surprisingly firm and unwrinkled neck. In one hand she carried a red, quilted Chanel bag (too over-powering); the other arm held a white cat (too furry).

Charles moved closer to the great movie star, catching the scent of her perfume (too floral), and bowed as if to royalty. *"Bonjour, Madame,"* he gushed.

"Good morning," she responded in a voice that was low and warm. But her face was cold, chiseled: thin, arched eyebrows, large deep-set eyes, high hollow cheekbones, long straight nose, narrow bowed lips. She did, however, look like a woman in her fifties, instead of someone in her eighties. Her plastic surgeon must be *fantastique!*

"This is my housekeeper, Lucinda Lopez," the actress said, introducing the peasant woman who stood quietly nearby. "And my cat Talbert." She scratched the animal's neck, and it undulated in her arms. "Both go everywhere with me."

Charles gave the housekeeper a cursory look, then smiled as genuinely as he could at the cat, for a man who abhorred such creatures.

"Entrer?" he said with a flourish of a gesture.

Charles opened the glass door, and Simone Vedette went in, the housekeeper in tow. He followed, shutting and locking the door behind them.

"Elle est la-bas," he instructed, as the two women hesitated just inside; he pointed toward the back of the shop.

The movie star and Mexican woman headed that way, through the outer room which was just for the general public.

Charles had spent hours arranging this outer room knowing Simone would pass through it, displaying his creations just so . . . But the actress took no notice as she made her way along.

The housekeeper, however, ooohed and aaahed at this and that, which only caused him great irritation.

They went through a thick red-velvet curtain, tied back to one side. *"Asseyez-vous a la chaise, s'il vous plait,"* Charles smiled.

Simone Vedette looked at him blankly. "I don't speak French, young man," she said. "And I wish you'd stop."

Charles blinked. "But, I thought . . . I mean, your name. . . ."

"I was born in Brooklyn," she said simply.

Charles stood dumbfounded, then recovered and gestured grandly to a gilded satin-covered French Empire chair. "Won't you please sit down," he said.

The great star sat, the cat curled on her lap.

He didn't bother to offer the housekeeper a chair; she found herself a place next to a rack of clothes.

Charles stood before the actress, bending slightly toward her, pressing his hands together, prayer-like.

"I have designed for you the most incredibly exquisite gown!" he exclaimed, then paused for effect. "And after you wear it at the Academy Awards, the media will dispense with their traditional fashion dissection—what did Cher wear? Who designed Geena Davis' gown? Who cares? *No one,* not once you have been seen wearing . . . ."

"Yes, yes," the actress interrupted impatiently, but her curiosity was clearly piqued. "Please, bring it out!"

The white, fluffy cat on her lap looked up at him with bored blue eyes.

Eagerly Charles disappeared behind a large dressing screen, where the gown was hidden, displayed on a platformed mannequin. He gazed at the dress, his eyes gleaming like the six thousand sequins and pearls he had hand-sewn onto the sheer beige silk souffle.

The gown was worth twenty thousand; he would charge her forty.

Carefully, tenderly, Charles covered up the mannequin with a large gold lamé cloth. Then he rolled the platform out from behind the screen, positioning the statue in front of the actress.

With a smile, he slowly pulled on one end of the gold

material, teasingly, exposing the bottom of the drop-dead gorgeous gown, and then, with a *snap,* yanked it completely off.

Simone Vedette gasped.

Charles beamed, looking at the dress. It truly was his finest work. A masterpiece that would soon make his name synonymous with the likes of Dior, Valentino and Gaultier!

His eyes went back to the actress who was still gasping, leaning forward, but now clutching her chest. The cat on her lap rose to its feet, struggling to keep from falling.

"Madame!" Charles cried out, alarmed. Something was wrong with the woman!

From behind him, the housekeeper shrieked, further terrifying the cat which leapt from his mistress' lap onto the mannequin, claws bared, clinging, ripping as it slid down the delicate material, sequins and pearls popping and dropping onto the floor, where the last of the legends now lay—no longer living.

Charles stared in shock and disbelief at the dead woman at his feet. Had he been foiled by his own brilliance? Had he finally done it?

Created a dress to die for?

Brenda Vedette sat in a leather chair in a posh office on Wilshire Boulevard in Beverly Hills.

The woman, in her mid-thirties, attractive, with straight, shoulder-length blonde hair, was dressed in a dark grey suit, an inexpensive copy of a Paris original. Across from her, behind a massive mahogany desk, was Mitchell Levin, a slender, bespectacled man in his sixties, who was her late mother's lawyer.

Brenda pulled a pack of cigarettes from her purse. "Mind if I smoke?" she asked.

By way of an answer, the lawyer pushed a glass ashtray toward her on the desk.

She lit the cigarette, took a puff, and blew the smoke out the side of her mouth. Then she asked, "So am I cut out of the will, or what?"

Mitchell Levin looked down at the document before him. "No," he said cautiously, "you aren't. However, there are a few provisions. . . ."

Brenda laughed hoarsely. "Like what? I find a job, get married, quit smoking?"

The corners of the lawyer's mouth turned up slightly, but more from disgust, Brenda thought, than amusement.

"These provisions," he explained, "have to do with your mother's cat Talbert and housekeeper, Lucinda Lopez."

A sickening feeling spread slowly through Brenda's body. *That crazy old broad hadn't left the bulk of everything to them, had she?*

Brenda took another puff of the cigarette and said as blandly as she could, "Go on."

Mitchell studied the papers in his hands. "It was your mother's wish that Talbert remain at her home in Malibu in the comfort he has been used to, and under the care of Lucinda, until his death, at which time the estate will go to you."

Brenda sat numbly and said nothing.

Mitchell said, "Now, you can *try* to contest the will, but I'm warning you. . . ."

"Mr. Levin!" Brenda snapped, working indignation into those few words, and the ones that followed. "I have no intention of going against my mother's wishes!"

Most likely prepared for a fight, the lawyer looked a little stunned.

Brenda leaned forward and forcefully stubbed her cigarette out in the ashtray. "My mother and I may not have seen eye to eye, but she certainly has the right to do whatever she wants with her money."

Brenda sat back in her chair, lowered her voice. "And she was correct in being concerned about Talbert . . . I wouldn't have wanted him. And I'd have sold the house. It holds nothing but painful memories for me." Her voice cracked at the end.

There was an awkward silence. Tears sprang to her eyes.

"Do you think it was easy being raised in the shadow of the great Simone Vedette?" Brenda blurted. "She *never* should have adopted me . . . She just didn't have the right temperament! And she was *too old*."

Brenda looked down at her hands in her lap, and shook her head slowly. "My mother expected so much from me, yet gave so little in return. I guess that was why I wrote the book . . . Any attention I could get from her, no matter how negative, was better than nothing."

"It hurt her deeply," the lawyer said.

"Well, *she* hurt *me!*"

Brenda sobbed into her hands.

Mitchell Levin reached into his coat pocket and pulled out a handkerchief. "Here," he said softly, giving it to her. "Use this."

Brenda dabbed at her eyes with the cloth. Composed herself. Looked at the lawyer. "I just want you to know, I did love my mother, and I'm sorry that book was ever published. And I'll certainly comply with any of her last wishes."

Mitchell gave Brenda a little smile; it seemed genuine. "Your mother would have been proud to hear you say that," he told her.

Brenda nodded. Then, as an afterthought, she asked, "Oh

. . . my monthly stipend . . . will it continue?"

"The same as usual."

The young woman stood. "Then if there's nothing else. . . ."

Mitchell rose from behind his desk. "Good-bye, Brenda," he said, extending one hand. "I'll be in touch. Take care of yourself."

"Thank you," she returned warmly, and shook his hand.

Out on the street, Brenda got into her five-year-old Ford Escort convertible, which was parked at the curb. She plucked any old cassette from the many tapes scattered on the seat next to her, and inserted it into the dash. Then with disco music throbbing, pulled out into the traffic.

She looked at herself in the visor mirror.

Her mother wasn't the only Vedette who could give an Academy Award performance. . . .

So she wouldn't get her inheritance until the cat was dead? Fine. How long could a cat live, anyway?

After all, accidents did happen.

A dark-haired woman in sunglasses, T-shirt, backpack and jeans walked her dog along the beach in Malibu, where expensive ocean-front homes crowded so close together they almost touched, with barely enough room between them for the fences that separated these patches of precious, puny real estate.

It was early afternoon, and anyone who might notice the young lady would not give her a second thought—even though the dog on the leash was a vicious pit bull—because the woman was carrying two socially and ecologically correct items: a pooper-scooper and a sack.

The dog seemed well behaved, stopping occasionally to sniff at this and that. The man the woman had bought the pit bull from had said the animal liked people . . . it was just *cats* the dog hated.

Be-wigged Brenda let the dog lead her down a narrow passageway between the tall wooden fences of two homes.

She stopped by the fence belonging to the house on the right. Quietly she pulled back a board she had loosened late last night.

She peeked through.

Talbert—that fat lazy puss—was having his usual afternoon nap on the patio. He lay on his side, in the shade of a tall potted plant, legs stretched out, dead to the world—and soon would be. The housekeeper was nowhere in sight.

Brenda unleashed the pit bull and gently pushed its head toward the opening in the fence.

The dog resisted at first, but then suddenly it caught sight of the sleeping cat, and with powerful legs propelled itself through the opening, splintering the wood, leaving an outline of its massive body on the remaining boards, moving like a freight train into the yard.

Brenda wanted to watch, but didn't dare. She stayed only long enough, hidden behind the wooden fence, to hear the snarls of the dog, and yowls of the cat, and then screams of the housekeeper who must have come running out of the house. . . .

Brenda hurried along the passageway between the fences, putting on a red nylon jacket, the pooper-scooper and leash, along with the black wig, hidden in the backpack.

Quickly she moved down the beach—just a pretty, blonde power-walker out for some exercise. A half a mile away, off Pacific Coast Highway, was her parked convertible.

Throwing the backpack in the back seat, she got in, and started the car. She grabbed a tape from off the passenger seat, and stuck it in the player.

Think I'll go over to Cartier and get that diamond tennis bracelet I've always wanted, she mused to herself.

"After all," she said aloud, smiling, driving off, the music of the Bee Gees blaring, "I can afford it now."

Later that night, under a sky bedecked with a million dazzling stars (though not as dazzling as the diamonds on her wrist), Brenda pulled the convertible into the driveway of her late mother's house.

She got out and pressed a buzzer on the gate of the wooden fence.

After a moment an intercom speaker crackled and Lucinda's voice said, "Yes? Who is it?"

The housekeeper sounded weary.

"It's Brenda. I've come to get a book."

There was a long pause. Then, "Okay. I let you in."

Brenda waited for the buzzer, and pushed open the gate.

She walked slowly by the patio which was awash in outside lighting. Everything appeared normal. No disturbed deck furniture, or over-turned potted plants. Even the fence had been repaired. It was as if nothing had ever happened.

But as Brenda approached the back door of the beach house, she noticed a dark stain on the patio cement.

Blood, perhaps?

She repressed a smile, as the housekeeper opened the door for her.

"Hello, Lucinda," Brenda said, as she entered the house. She was standing in a comfortable, tastefully decorated TV room. It was where her mother had spent most of her time.

"I need to find a book a friend loaned me," Brenda explained. "She wants it back, and I think I gave it to my mother."

The housekeeper stared at her with large liquid eyes behind her old-fashioned glasses.

"Is something wrong?" Brenda asked, feigning concern. "You don't look well."

"This . . . this afternoon," the woman began haltingly, "a terrible thing happened."

"What?"

"A big dog got through the fence and attacked little Talbert!"

"No!" Brenda said, aghast. "How awful!"

"I called the police, and they had to *shoot* the dog."

"How horrible!" Lucinda shook her head slowly, then looked down at the floor. "That poor, poor cat . . . What a cruel way for it to die."

"Oh, Talbert's not dead," the housekeeper said.

"Not dead?"

Lucinda pointed to other side of room, where Brenda now saw the cat, sleeping on a pet-bed on the floor next to a chair. Several of his paws were bandaged.

"He got away from that bad dog," Lucinda explained, "and climbed the . . . what do you call it? On the side of the house?"

"Challis," Brenda said flatly.

"*Si.* The challis. We're lucky it was there."

"Yes," Brenda replied slowly. "Lucky."

The room fell silent.

"You don't have to worry about Talbert, Miss Brenda," Lucinda said firmly. "From now on, I'm not letting him out of my sight."

Brenda smiled weakly.

The housekeeper smiled back. "Now, what was the name of that book you wanted?"

It was hot in the tiny, dingy apartment on Alameda Street,

but the air conditioner in the window wasn't plugged in.

Brenda stood by the dirt-streaked window looking down on the filthy street below. She had rented the third floor room, directly over the building's entrance, three weeks ago, under an assumed name.

She stepped back a little from the window as a limousine pulled up at the curb.

The chauffeur got out and went around to the side of the car, where he helped Lucinda out of the back seat. She was wearing her usual cotton housedress and headscarf, and was carrying a sack of groceries, which she brought every Saturday morning to her elderly mother who lived below, on the first floor. Looped around one arm was a green leash, and at the end of the leash, was Talbert.

The housekeeper made her way leisurely up the sidewalk of the apartment building.

She climbed the short flight of steps, bag in both arms, the leashed Talbert trailing behind.

Brenda, her head pressed against the dirty windowpane, watched until the moment Lucinda disappeared from view into the building, Talbert bringing up the rear. Then Brenda opened the window further and shoved the massive air conditioner out.

It crashed on the steps below, making a terrible metallic racket, the leash winding out from under it like a green tail.

Brenda shut the window, gently.

In the late afternoon, as the sun descended on Malibu, shimmering on the ocean like tinsel on a tree, Brenda wheeled her convertible into the driveway of her mother's house.

She got out, carrying a small basket, and rang the buzzer.

She had a present for Talbert, Brenda told the house-keeper, and could she come in?

Inside the TV room, Brenda's eyes darted to the little cat bed on the floor by the chair, but it was empty.

"The pet store around the corner from me is going out of business," Brenda said to Lucinda, "and everything was half-price." She paused and held up the basket in her hand. "I thought Talbert might like these treats, and cat-nip, and stuff."

Lucinda looked at her sadly.

Brenda let her mouth fall open. "Don't tell me something else has happened to Talbert!" she said incredulously.

The housekeeper nodded.

"What?"

"An air conditioner fell down on him."

"An *air conditioner?*"

Lucinda told her what had happened.

"That is so incredible!" Brenda said, then added, sadly, "I'm going to miss that sweet, little animal. . . ."

"Oh, he's all right," the housekeeper said.

"All right?"

"Because the air conditioner fell on the steps," Lucinda explained, "there was a little space for him. It did hurt his tail, though."

Perhaps hearing his name, the white Persian entered the room from the kitchen. His front paws were still bandaged, and now so was his tail.

Brenda glared at the cat.

Lucinda bent down, gently picked up the animal, and kissed his diffident face. "It must be true what they say," the housekeeper said, speaking more to the animal than Brenda. "A cat does have nine lives."

In her convertible, Brenda ejected the cassette out of the

player, snatched another off the passenger seat, and shoved it inside.

"That mangy beast doesn't have nine lives," she fumed, "he has *ten!*"

She tore out of the driveway, tires squealing, music cranked.

Maybe she needed something so lethal it would snuff out every last life fat Talbert had left. It was time to stop playing Wily Coyote to his Road Runner.

Time for something a little more high-tech. . . .

Brenda bought a modem, and hooked it up to her home computer. Then she joined the Internet and, going through an anonymous server known as a double-blind to protect her identity, posted this message: *Looking for way to kill neighbor's evil, annoying cat. Will pay $1,000. Signed, Sleepless in LA.*

Within hours, her computer began to beep as hundreds of responses poured in from all over the world; evidently, a lot of cat haters traveled the information highway in cyberspace. She heard from a terrorist group in Tangier who wanted the money for guns, and a Russian physicist suggesting she use red mercury—the latest in modern warfare, and some nut from New York who offered to do the job for free. . . .

But the message that intrigued her the most, read: *Acme Electronics, 555 Acme Rd., Cupertino (Silicon Valley). Come after hours. Bring tape of the cat's meowing.*

This person seemed serious.

"But it's a mouse!" Brenda said disappointedly, looking at the small brown rodent on the workbench in the cluttered back room of the electronic store.

"A *robot* mouse," corrected the middle-aged man who had introduced himself as Steve. He was about average height and weight, with sandy hair and a close-cropped beard; not the skinny, nerdy-type with glasses Brenda had expected.

Brenda's eyes widened. "*That's* a robot?"

The man nodded. "You've heard of robot bugs?" he asked.

Brenda shook her head, no.

"They're miniature robots used mostly for espionage, but they don't really look like bugs." He paused and affectionately caressed the mouse's back. "This is my genius. It can squeeze under doors, scurry around in the heat ducts, hide under the furniture—just like a real mouse—only there's one little difference . . . This one explodes."

"Cool," Brenda said.

He looked at her sharply, eyes as brown as the mouse. "Did you bring the cassette?" he asked.

She nodded and dug into her purse and handed him the tape she had made of the cat meowing; she had recorded it the day before when she went over to sunbathe on the patio.

"Oh, and I have the money," Brenda added. She reached in her jacket pocket and pulled out ten one-hundred-dollar bills and put them on the workbench.

He smiled, but the smile was lop-sided. "That's good," he said, "but it won't be enough . . . Brenda."

A chill went up her back. She hadn't given him her real name. And her identity on her computer message was supposed to have been kept secret!

"I cracked your anonymous I.D.," he shrugged. "Anyone who hides behind a double-blind has something to hide, I always say. Next time protect yourself with a password."

Brenda felt her face grow hot. She didn't know what to say.

"I also accessed your home computer files," he continued.

"*Which* files?" she demanded.

" 'Dear Monica, I won't get my inheritance until the cat is dead . . . ' "

Brenda grabbed the money off the workbench and bolted for the door. But the man beat her to it, blocking the exit.

"Get out of my way, or I'll scream!" she shouted.

He put both hands up in the air. "Whoa! I'm not going to touch you . . . I just want a little more money, that's all."

She backed away from him. Narrowed her eyes. "How *much* more?"

He lowered his hands. "Ten thousand."

"Ten thousand!" she said, almost choking on the words. "I haven't got that kind of money!"

"But you *will* have," he said slyly. "That and a lot more. . . ."

She stared at him.

"Look," he explained, his voice softer, "that robot is worth five grand, easy. I'll need to replace it. And then I want to build another."

She considered that, vacillating. The robot mouse *was* a neat gizmo, she thought, and would certainly do the trick.

But then she had a few more thoughts. Blowing the cat to Kingdom Come wouldn't exactly look like an accidental death. She would certainly be suspected. . . .

Brenda looked at Steve, who was grinning at her smugly.

But the authorities could only get to her through him . . . and he *already* knew too much.

"Okay," she agreed, "I'll pay you ten thousand. But not until I get *my* money. Then you'll get *yours*."

That would give her enough time to figure out how to kill him.

She made a mental note to remember to ask for the tape of the cat back . . . wouldn't want any evidence left behind.

"Deal." He smiled and held out his hand for her to shake,

which she did. "Now, let me show you how this cute little mouse works."

A tiny sliver of moon hung high in the sky, like the slit of a sleeping cat's eye, as Brenda drove her convertible slowly along the highway in front of her mother's house.

She parked the car in the mouth of the driveway and got out.

In the stillness of the night, she crept along the garage. She bent to the ground and carefully removed the mouse from her jacket pocket and placed the small robot on the cement, underneath the fence, between the boards and the ground.

There the mouse would stay, tucked away, for however long it took, until the cat meowed. The robot would then identify that particular sound, and with the guidance of a heat-seeking device, zero in on the animal and blow it to smithereens.

She smiled at the irony of a mouse chasing a cat—and killing it.

Brenda walked back to her car and slid in behind the wheel. She stuck a tape in the player, started the car.

"MEOW!" said the speakers.

Brenda froze, realizing what she had done. She looked over quickly to the space under the fence where she had put the mouse.

Even in the darkness she could see the small rodent move out of its hiding place and cut a path right toward her.

Brenda floored the car's accelerator, and with tires squealing and rubber smoking, backed out of the driveway and speed off.

She could outrun it, she thought. *After all, how fast could a little mouse go?*

Brenda flew down the highway, then suddenly she

slammed on her breaks and made a "U" turn, her tires squealing, as she bumped up on the curb, nearly running over a derelict who was sifting through a garbage can.

That should throw the little vermin off, she thought.

Furtively, she glanced over her shoulder. Under the bright streetlights, she saw the small brown mouse make a tiny "U" turn of its own, still tracking her, closing in.

Brenda went faster, her car careening, taking Malibu Canyon Road at a dangerous speed, the vehicle twisting and turning, as it slid sideways into a pole.

The impact knocked Brenda nearly unconscious. But she did manage to say, "Oh, shit."

And there wasn't time for another word, before her world flashed white, then red, then black. . . .

"Mas vino, madre?" Lucinda asked, a wine decanter in her hand.

"Por favor," her mother answered. The woman, slender, with short, silver-grey hair, leaned forward in her lounge chair on the patio, and held out a crystal goblet toward her daughter.

Lucinda filled the glass with Chateau Latour, and as she did, her mother told her in Spanish how beautiful Lucinda looked in the dress that she was wearing.

Lucinda smiled. She *did* feel like a movie star in the beige gown with sequins and pearls! If Talbert hadn't ripped it, she never would have owned the dress. So upset was Mr. Charles that he just gave it to her! And the rips that she hand-sewed shut herself hardly even showed, much.

Whenever she wore the dress—usually with one of her colorful headscarves and sandals—she proudly told whoever would listen that the gown was designed by Chez Charles on Rodeo Drive. It was the least she could do for that nice man!

Lucinda looked over at the sleeping white cat, stretched out on the patio. Held in its paws was the little pouch of catnip that Brenda had given him.

Poor Brenda, thought the housekeeper, *Whatever had the girl been up to the night she died in that fiery crash just a few miles away?* The police said there had been a witness. A poor man without a home saw the whole thing. He claimed Brenda was killed by a mouse that chased her down the highway! But, of course, that was silly.

A portable phone on the patio table rang and Lucinda picked it up.

"Hello?" she said.

"Miss Lopez?" a male voice asked.

"Yes?"

"This is Harold Davis, from Harold's Pet Emporium," he said. "Got a male white Persian for you."

"*Gracias,* Mr. Davis," Lucinda replied, "but I won't be needing the cat now." She paused, then added, "However, if I *should* want another in the future, can you get me one as fast as you got me the other two?"

To Kill a Cat

It had been a year since Maggie's husband died.

Tom's cruel death of pancreatic cancer came quickly; and yet was kind enough to allow him time to fully appreciate life, and say goodbye to friends.

In his final days he seemed at peace, in his drugged semi-coma, surrounded by loving family members.

He had the easy part—dying—while Maggie was left living with sadness and guilt that drove her to the brink of suicide.

Unable to teach, she took a leave of absence from the college, and sought professional help to cope with her grief.

Now, buoyed by time, she had the strength to visit the park where Tom proposed to her fifteen years ago. Beneath this stone bridge, on the grassy bank of the pond, surrounded by weeping willows, he had kissed her and promised never to leave.

She stood there, in the dusk of a cool summer evening, and stared out at the water. The branches of the willows, blown by the wind, reached out, as if to comfort her.

But she did not weep.

She'd come up from the depths of depression, to break its hold and gasp for air. She wanted to live—though she knew she would never forget the helplessness of standing by, watching someone die.

Perhaps that was why she reacted as she did, when something sailed off the bridge and splashed into the pond. For an instant, she thought it was a sack of garbage, and looked up sharply toward the bridge in disgust.

In the darkness, she saw no one. The sack—which was beginning to sink—was squirming; an unearthly screech came from within.

Something *live* was in it!

The water was cold, the pond, surprisingly deep. Weeds grabbing at her legs threatened to hold her back. Her jeans and sweater, heavy and cumbersome, slowed her down.

The sack had gone under.

Reaching out in the water, Maggie searched with her hands, but found nothing. Then she kicked with her feet, and felt it!

Quickly, she yanked the sack to the surface, and putting it on the back of her head and shoulders, held it there with one hand as she swam back to shore with the other.

On the bank, on her knees, she tore off the twine that sealed the burlap bag, and emptied it.

A large black cat lay lifeless.

Rhythmically, she pushed on its swollen stomach.

The cat didn't move. Instinctively, she grabbed its hind legs, held the animal upside down like a newborn baby, and shook it!

Water streamed from its mouth, and the cat sputtered and spasmed as it fought its way back from the dead.

Maggie cried out with joy and relief as the terrified animal clung to her.

"Meow! Meow!" it shrieked. "Meow! Meow!"

"There, there," she soothed, holding it tightly, rocking slightly. "There, there."

For a moment she stayed on her knees, caressing the trembling cat. Then she stood up with it. Outraged.

"Who would *do* such a thing?" she said loudly, angrily, for the benefit of a person who had long since fled.

She gazed down into the cat's golden eyes. "Who would do such a thing?" she repeated softly, sadly.

The cat said nothing, clinging to her, its claws buried in Maggie's soaked sweater.

Maggie shivered, as much from the thought some bastard could be so sadistic, as from her damp, cold clothes.

"I'm taking you home!" she said to the cat, firmly, indignantly. She bent down and picked up the sack and twine, then walked toward her car, her tennis shoes sloshing as she went.

She opened the trunk and threw in the burlap bag and twine—perhaps later they might be useful in locating the owner and bringing that vile person to justice! Then Maggie pulled out a stadium blanket and wrapped herself up with the cat and got behind the wheel of her car and drove home, the animal quivering against her.

In the spacious kitchen of her Victorian house, Maggie stood at the stove in a terry-cloth robe, stirring a pan of hot chicken soup.

The cat was on the floor, next to the round oak table, in a large box Maggie found in the basement. She thought the arrangement best, as she'd never had a pet, and wasn't sure *what* to expect.

She gave the cat a bowl of the soup—cooled down with tap water—and it greedily ate.

After cleaning up the dishes, Maggie went off to bed, leaving a small light on in the kitchen for her guest.

Soon she fell into a deep, deep sleep . . . at first restful, then suddenly filled with delirious dreams of witches and goblins and demons from hell. . . .

If she could only wake up! In the distant corner of her subconscious she recognized the barking of her neighbor's dog—the yapping was a nightly annoyance she tried to ignore, but now she fought her way toward it. In the limbo-land of half-asleep, her eyes lidded, she sensed the presence of something.

Large glowing eyes stared into hers.

She sat up in bed. She looked around. Had she imagined it? A movement caught her eye. But it was just the curtains being tossed about from the brisk night air coming in the open window.

In the kitchen, the cat lay sleeping, curled in a ball, its back rising and falling peacefully. Maggie returned to her bedroom.

With a sigh, she crawled under the quilts and closed her eyes. She needed a good night's sleep! Tomorrow she had to find the nice cat a new home.

Maggie had driven by the sign a hundred times, but had never given it much thought; now she followed the directions and turned off the highway onto a blacktop that led out of town.

The brilliant morning sun streaked in the car window across the cat that lay on the front seat, making its black coat shine. Maggie looked at the cat and smiled, happy about the good deed she was about to perform.

After several miles the black top ended and Maggie slowed as the road turned to gravel. Though her tires kicked up dust, she kept the windows down, reveling in the smell of ripening cornfields that had just begun to turn brown.

Another sign appeared, and she turned off the gravel and into the grassy lane of the County Animal Shelter. To her right, enclosed by a low, rustic wooden fence, was a pet cemetery. Each of the tiny graves had its own little marker, and many were decorated with plastic flowers. Butterflies danced among them.

To her left loomed a white metal building, and Maggie pulled her car up to it and shut off the engine.

The cat, alert, began to stiffen, its ears rotating forward. Maggie picked it up and its claws dug into the soft fabric of her shirt.

The cat made a pitiful noise.

"It's all right," Maggie answered cheerfully, getting out of the car. "They're going to help us."

Inside the building, the sounds and smells of the caged animals assaulted her. The cat dug in further, and Maggie had to hold it tightly to keep it from clawing all the way up to the top of her head.

A young woman with puffy blond hair and ratted-up bangs sat behind a metal desk just inside the door. She was reading a book, and looked up from it. Her features were so perfect, so completely void of anything unique or interesting, that Maggie felt if she ever saw the woman again she would never recognize her.

"I have a cat," Maggie said, raising her voice above the din of the yapping, yowling animals.

"Uh-huh," the woman said, putting the book down.

"I hope you can find it a home."

The woman eyed her slowly. "You don't want to keep it?" she asked.

"Well . . . no," Maggie said, taken slightly aback. "I don't *want* a pet. That's why I'm here."

The woman sighed, seemingly annoyed, and opened a drawer. She pulled out a form and picked up a pencil. "Where did you find it?" she asked flatly.

"In the pond," Maggie answered. "At the park." Then she added, somewhat sanctimoniously, "*Someone* tried to *drown* it."

The young woman stopped writing, and said almost

smugly, "Maybe you didn't do it a favor."

"What do you mean?" Maggie demanded, bristling a little. The woman sat back in her chair and crossed her legs, showing large holes in the knees of her jeans. "We got room for just eighteen cats here," she explained. "About forty come in every week." The young woman paused. "If we're *lucky* we give away two."

Maggie stared at her and clutched the cat tighter. "What happens to the rest?" she asked.

The woman didn't answer, but looked past Maggie and hollered, "Rusty!"

Maggie turned to see a thin young man in shorts and a T-shirt. On his shirt was a picture of a heavy metal rock group, with the word "Megadeth" above it. The kid had a face full of freckles and small eyes with no eyebrows at all. Strands of unruly red hair stuck out from under a baseball cap he wore backward on his head.

"Rusty," the young woman said, "put the cat some-where—*anywhere*—until we can find it a cage."

"Okay," he answered dully. He reached for the cat, and pulled it off Maggie, and the animal's claws caught in her blouse, undoing one button, revealing her lacy white bra.

Rusty grinned, showing sharp little teeth.

Maggie glared back, clutching her shirt closed, and watched as he left with the cat, down the cement corridor, disappearing through a door beyond which she glimpsed caged animals. Then she turned to the woman.

"You will *try* to find the cat a home?" Maggie asked. It was more a statement than a question.

The young woman nodded indifferently, her lips a tight sullen line.

"It's a *nice* cat," Maggie defended.

"It's a male Bombay," the young woman said coldly.

"They're not all that friendly."

Now this upset Maggie, and the woman, seeing she'd gone too far, and perhaps sensing she might get into trouble, tried her best to look sincere. "But we'll do what we can," the young woman promised.

Maggie was hesitant.

"You check back with us at the end of the week, if you like," the woman suggested.

"Yes," Maggie said, brightening. "Yes, I'll do that." Then she dug into her purse and found a twenty-dollar bill. "I want to make a donation," she said, holding out the money.

"Thank you," the young woman said, taking it, smiling at last. "We do rely on donations."

Maggie nodded, and left.

Getting into her car, she wondered if the twenty would buy pet food or hair spray. But it just didn't matter. It bought Maggie relief from the guilt she felt as she drove out of the lane, leaving the cat behind, not looking at the pet cemetery as she went by.

At home, Maggie vacuumed the Oriental rug in the living room—something she'd have to do constantly if she had a cat. Then she dusted the Queen Anne furniture she inherited from her grandmother; its delicate needlepoint would never survive destructive sharp claws.

But in the hallway, while polishing the mirror, she stopped, rag suspended in mid-air as she stared at the reflection of the cat's box, behind her, still in the kitchen.

"What's the matter?" she sneered at herself. "Are you afraid to love even a *cat?*"

She threw down the rag, and ran out the door and got in her car.

In a race against time—it was late and the shelter soon

would be closing—Maggie sped along the country road, dust encompassing the car, and, before long, wheeled into its grassy lane only to have to throw on her brakes.

In front of the building the red lights of a police car and ambulance were flashing.

Puzzled, Maggie rolled down her dirty car window to see better, and slowly pulled off to the side, next to the cemetery. She shut off the engine and got out.

Quietly she entered the building.

"I don't know *how* it happened!" the young woman was wailing; so cool and collected earlier, she was now quite hysterical.

"Just take it slow," said a policeman who stood near the woman. He made a calm-down gesture with both hands.

The young woman breathed deeply, composing herself, then looked at the cop with wet, mascara-blackened eyes.

"He was getting ready to do some dogs," she said in a quavering voice. "We use gas pellets and . . ." She halted and swallowed thickly.

"Go on," the cop said.

"When I hadn't seen him for awhile, I went looking . . ." Now she stared down at her feet, her face contorting. "Somehow the door must have *closed,* locking him in!"

The young woman buried her face in her hands and sobbed, "Christ! It shouldn't happen to a dog."

"Excuse me," Maggie said from the doorway.

The young woman looked over at her with the eyes of a startled animal.

The cop took a step toward Maggie. "Ma'am, you're going to have to leave," he ordered.

"I came back for my cat," Maggie said speaking to the woman who continued to stare.

"I'm sorry if I've come at a bad time," Maggie continued,

undeterred, "but I want that cat before you do anything to it."

"Lady," the young woman said, her eyes now half-crazed, "there's nobody *to* do anything to it!"

"I'm going to ask you just once more to *leave*," the policeman barked.

Intimidated, Maggie backed out the of building, and for a moment stood off to one side in the grass, indecisive about what to do next, when the front door of the shelter flew open.

Two men came out carrying a stretcher. Maggie watched them, rather detached—the cat, after all, was her main concern—as they made their way to the ambulance. The men didn't seem to be in much of a hurry.

But suddenly Maggie realized that the stretcher was *covered;* underneath she could make out a form. With mounting horror she stared, unable to look away. As the gurney was lifted into the back of the van it got jostled.

The blanket slipped. Red hair sprung out from under.

Rusty.

Maggie stumbled back a few steps, then turned and fled to her car. She opened the door and quickly got in.

On the front seat, sleeping serenely, was the cat.

"Kitty!" she cried, her horror turning to joy. "Oh, Kitty!"

She reached for the cat. "But how . . . ?" she began, then burst into tears. "Forgive me," she whispered, her face lost in its fur.

Then she started the car, turned it around, and tore out of the lane, burying the pet cemetery in a cloud of dust.

Maggie stood anxiously in the reception area of the Animal Care Clinic, a rambling wooden affair that looked more like a lodge than a pet hospital. It was located just a few miles outside of town, on an old winding road that ran along the river. The clinic was owned by Dr. Goodman and his wife Edna.

"I hope I didn't do the wrong thing," Maggie sighed.

Dr. Goodman smiled reassuringly. "I don't think so," he said. He was a stout man in his sixties, with white hair and kind eyes that were made even kinder by the magnification of his glasses. Maggie knew him from church where he sang in the choir with a vibrant yet compassionate voice, traits she had heard he brought to his work with animals.

"Although," the doctor admitted, nodding his head slightly, "there are those who think differently—cat experts who say this kind of thing should never be done."

Maggie frowned.

"However," Dr. Goodman continued, "if it means that a cat might be adopted instead of put to sleep. . . ."

A door in the back of the reception area opened and a portly, attractive woman entered. She had short grey hair and round, rosy cheeks that dimpled as she smiled.

She was carrying Maggie's cat.

"Ah, here's Edna now," the doctor said. Maggie smiled as Mrs. Goodman came toward her; but the smile vanished when she got a closer look at her pet.

"Oh dear," Maggie said, concerned, "what's wrong with him?"

"It's just the effects of the anesthesia," Dr. Goodman said. "He'll be fine in a couple of hours."

"But his paws . . ." Maggie said, gesturing to the cat's bandaged feet. ". . . I didn't think they had to be . . ."

"We like to wrap them for protection and to keep the incisions clean," the doctor explained. "You may untape them in a few days."

Maggie gingerly took the cat from Mrs. Goodman; the animal felt limp in her arms.

"Just let him sleep," the doctor advised. Maggie nodded slowly.

"You can call us if you have any questions," his wife added helpfully. "We're here until nine o'clock tonight."

Maggie thanked them and left.

She put the cat in the car on the front seat, right next to her, but it crawled away in slow motion, toward the opposite door, and turned itself around until its back was to her.

Maggie drove home, feeling rejected, thinking that she shouldn't have had the cat de-clawed.

In the kitchen, she put the cat on the floor, on a special pillow she had bought for its homecoming; but after a minute, it stood unsteadily, and moved away, and staggered like a drunk into the bedroom to be alone.

Maggie felt heartsick.

Later, around suppertime, when Maggie was cooking some fish, the cat emerged from seclusion, and, walking quite well on its bandaged paws, joined her by the stove. Relieved, Maggie bent down to pet it.

"Feeling better?" Maggie smiled, feeling better.

She put some of the fish on a plate, and set it down on the floor and watched as the cat ravenously ate. When it was done, it went to the back door, and meowed. Maggie complied, and the cat went out.

After Maggie had finished washing the dishes, she stepped outside and called for the cat.

But it didn't come.

She looked around the yard, but saw no sign of it.

Now Maggie began to worry—twilight had arrived—and she frantically searched up and down the street. When that failed to produce her pet, she alerted her neighbors who promised to call her if they should see the cat.

In her kitchen, Maggie paced back and forth, looking out

the back door every fifteen minutes or so. Darkness closed in. Sometime after nine, a siren pierced the peaceful night like a knife, then grew distant as the vehicle headed out of town. Except for that, all was quiet—even the Doberman pinscher next door.

Maggie set the cat's pillow out on the stoop, and—leaving the porch light on—locked the back door. Then she went off to bed.

Her rest was fitful at best, however, and during the night she got up and peered out the window; she could see the little pillow from there. . . .

But it lay empty.

In the morning, she awoke with a start, and jumped out of bed as if guilty for having slept, and ran to the window.

The cat was curled up on the pillow!

Her heart pounding, robe flapping, bare feet slapping the floor, Maggie ran to the kitchen and flung open the door.

"Where have you been?" she practically shouted.

The cat looked up. Unperturbed.

"Never mind," Maggie sighed bending down to get it. "I'm just glad you're home."

Then she held the cat out. "But just look at you!" she scolded. "You're full of cockleburs and . . . oh! Your paws!"

The bandages on its front feet were ragged and filthy. Maggie took the cat into the hallway and picked up the phone. "I'm going to call the vet!" she said, and dialed the number with her free hand.

A woman's voice answered; it wasn't Mrs. Goodman.

"Dr. Goodman, please," said Maggie urgently.

"I'm afraid all calls to our Animal Care Clinic are being referred to another veterinarian service."

"But I want to talk to Dr. Goodman," Maggie insisted.

There was a pause. "I'm afraid that's not possible."

"Why?" Maggie asked.

The voice, now softer, said, "The doctor and his wife were in an automobile accident last night."

"Oh, no!" Maggie moaned. She set the cat down. "Please . . . tell me. . . ."

"On their way home from the clinic they lost control of their car and ran into a guard rail, broke through and went into the river."

"Dear God," Maggie gasped. "What could have happened?"

"According to Mrs. Goodman, an animal ran onto the road in front of them and the doctor swerved so they wouldn't hit it."

Maggie looked down at the cat, licking one half-bandaged front paw, its pink tongue darting. "A deer, perhaps?" she asked weakly.

"Something much smaller," the woman said, then sighed. "I'm afraid the doctor was more concerned about saving the animal's life than saving his own. So typical of him. . . ."

"What do you mean?" said Maggie, alarmed. "Dr. Goodman's all right, isn't he?" Out of the corner of her eye she saw the cat, trotting off to the bedroom, head high, tail erect, bandages trailing behind.

"Dr. Goodman drowned."

Maggie hummed a little tune as she set the dining room table with her best crystal and china. When she had finished, she stepped back, and surveyed her work.

She smiled, then frowned.

"What should I use for a centerpiece?" she asked the cat.

The cat, lying on a window seat nearby, basking in the rays of the fading, late afternoon sun, stretched out its body and flexed its paws, which had healed nicely in the past week.

Maggie went to the cat and wagged a finger in its face. "Now I want you to be on your *best* behavior," she warned. "This is a colleague of mine. A *professor!*"

The cat yawned, unimpressed. Maggie leaned over the animal and opened the window.

"It would be *so* nice to have some fresh air," she said, looking out.

But the woman next door and her two little girls were having a picnic in their back yard, which was adjacent to Maggie's. The children yelled and screamed as they chased each other around with sticks. Their mother, a single parent in her thirties with short curly brown hair and a tired-looking face, was in the process of lighting a small candle on the table; she stopped and hollered at them. The family dog, chained nearby, determined not to be left out of the excitement, barked frantically, running in and out of his dog house, kicking up straw.

Maggie shut the window. "So much for *that* idea," she sighed.

The front doorbell chimed.

Maggie answered it, and greeted Professor Fudder, who stood uncomfortably in a three-piece suit. A bachelor in his early fifties with a close-cropped grey beard, he was holding a bouquet of roses.

"What beautiful flowers!" Maggie said, then added, "But you shouldn't have."

"Nonsense," the professor scoffed. "Merely a token of my gratitude for being invited to partake in your culinary delights."

"Thank you," Maggie smiled, amused. "I think." She gestured inside. "Please, come in, professor."

"Throckmorton," he corrected, stepping past her.

"Just make yourself at home . . . Throckmorton . . . while I put the roses in water."

She went into the kitchen, then returned with the flowers in a crystal vase, and set them on the table.

Maggie was surprised at how well the dinner went, considering her nervousness in preparing something she'd never served before, and to someone who had such gourmet tastes; but the professor really seemed to enjoy her appetizer of fried banana chips and entree of curried lamb with rice . . . and Maggie knew *nothing* could beat her mother's recipe for German chocolate pie.

The time passed quickly with shoptalk about their upcoming classes; Maggie told the professor she was anxious to return to teaching. When the conversation drifted to their pets—Maggie knew the professor had four cats—she suggested they leave the dishes in the dining room and move to the kitchen for coffee.

The professor took a seat at the oak table and Maggie went to get some cups from the cupboard. Out the window above the sink, she could see that the family next door had gone inside. The lone candle left flickering on the picnic table softly illuminated the doghouse in the night; the chain lead inside, indicating the animal had also retired. Maggie opened the window and let in the cool breeze.

"Professor . . . Throckmorton," she said, now pouring him a cup of coffee, "I wanted to find some way of re-paying you for taking over my classes last year when. . . ." She couldn't finish the sentence.

"No payment necessary," said the professor, jumping in graciously.

Maggie sat down and poured herself a cup. "I thought inviting you to dinner might be a nice way of saying thanks."

"You've provided the most delicious thank-you note I ever ate, my dear."

Maggie smiled, then stared down at her coffee. "I'm afraid I had another reason for inviting you here tonight."

"A hidden agenda? How delightful."

She nodded, running one finger around the rim of her cup. "I need to tap into your expertise. . . ."

The professor leaned forward, just slightly.

"Can cats kill the way people can kill?"

The professor blinked, and it seemed to Maggie that his face registered disappointment before taking on a look of puzzlement. "Come again?" he said.

"I know this may sound silly . . . but do you think it's possible for a cat to kill—maliciously, cunningly—like a human can kill?"

The professor sat back in his chair. "Well cats *are* extraordinary hunters . . ."

"I don't mean kill for food," Maggie interrupted. "I mean kill for *revenge*—or just the hell of it!"

The professor stared. "You can't be serious," he said, after a moment. "Have you been reading horror novels on your sabbatical?"

"What I've been reading," Maggie said, feeling her face begin to flush, "is that. . . ."

She shut her mouth. The cat, curled up by the stove, was watching them intently, as if it could understand their conversation. Maggie got up from the table and picked up the cat and put it out the back door, then returned to her chair.

"What I've been reading," she began again, almost in a whisper, "is that a kitten's mother will first bring back food to her babies and kill it in front of them, to teach them how. Then, she brings back prey for *them* to kill."

"Continue."

"Cats learn everything from their mothers—or *mother-substitutes:* humans that raise them from kittens."

"Point being?"

"Point being that a cat raised by Mother Teresa is going to be a very different animal than the one that learned the life-style of, say, mass-murderer John Wayne Gacy."

The professor laughed. "My dear," he said, "your conjecture is pure nonsense. Cats are not that intelligent. Furthermore, today's feline has remained close to its ancestral form; its behavior is still remarkably like the African wild cat from which it was gradually developed thousands of years ago."

"I don't agree," Maggie argued. "I think years of man-handling and coddling have caused the modern cat to forget most of its instincts, much less its purpose. And prolonged exposure to sophisticated human beings has perhaps spawned a new breed of cat—a much more intelligent and crafty animal than you can imagine."

"Hogwash, my dear."

"Then *how,* for example, do you explain the cat that learned to run a toy train on 'Stupid Pet Tricks'?" Maggie asked.

The professor opened his mouth to speak, but instead of words came a terrible screech, and it took Maggie a second or two before she realized that the shriek had not emanated from the professor at all, but from something outside. As the horrible screeching continued—she couldn't tell if it was man or beast—Maggie jumped out of her chair and ran to the back door and flung it open.

The night was blacker than Indian ink, but Maggie had no trouble seeing, because the doghouse in the yard next door lit up the sky.

It was aflame.

The Doberman pinscher—the source of the

screeching—raced back and forth, as far as the chain would take him, his body a torch. Perhaps in his doggy-mind he thought that action might help, but it only made things worse.

Maggie stood in frozen horror, one hand to her mouth, the other holding the door open, when suddenly her attention was diverted from the tragedy before her, as her cat shot out of the darkness, and moved swiftly up the steps, and past her, into the kitchen, on its way to the bedroom, no doubt.

She could not help the thought that popped into her head: *Now what have you done?*

The two little girls, hearing the commotion, came running out of their house and stopped a few feet away from the blazing fire. They held onto each other, jumping up and down like demented cheerleaders, their high-pitched screams blending together to make one continuous one, as they watched their beloved pet shudder and drop, its legs finally getting the message that the rest of it was dead.

Something touched Maggie and *she* jumped.

"I've called the fire department," the professor said, solemnly, one hand on her arm. "Come in and sit down. Nothing can help that poor beast now."

But Maggie moved away from him, toward the fire which had begun to die down, her eyes searching.

The candle on the picnic table was missing; knocked into the doghouse by a cat's paw . . . ?

Mercifully, the siren of the approaching fire truck drowned out the sobbing of the girls, and their mother, who had joined them, her arms around them both, head lowered in grief.

Maggie shrank back into the shadows, then moved on wobbly legs up the back steps and into the kitchen. She sat down numbly at the table.

"Maggie?" the professor asked, concerned. He was standing beside her, a hand lifted to, but not quite touching, her shoulder.

"I'm all right," she responded, not looking at him but through him. "I must ask you to go," she said softly.

"I'll telephone you later," he said.

She nodded.

He thanked her again for the dinner, but she hardly heard him; he found his way out, forgotten by his hostess.

She continued to sit until the cat came back, rubbing itself against her leg. She picked it up and kissed its face. "I love you," she whispered. "I really do."

Then she put it down and got up from the table and went outside.

A storm was coming; big drops of rain fell from the sky, hitting her face, running down it, mingling with her tears.

In the garage, she opened the trunk of her car, and pulled out the blanket that she had used to warm herself and the cat, what seemed like eons ago. For a moment, she held it to her cheek, tenderly, caressingly, like a baby's blanket. Then she let it fall back into the trunk, and reached in further, for the burlap bag and twine. . . .

It had been six months since Jim's wife left him—for a woman for God's sake! During that time he thought he would die from the pain and embarrassment she caused him. Only one thing kept him going: his nine-year-old son, Nate.

Sitting in the rowboat across from his dad, Nate was a small mirror image of his father. They'd been out fishing, cramming as much fun as they could into the last few days before school started, when the storm suddenly came up.

They'd taken refuge under the old stone bridge.

Now the rain had stopped, and the clouds parted showing

a brilliant moon, and they drifted out tentatively in the old rowboat.

Something hit the water, off the stern, splashing them both. Jim had only to reach out to haul it in, whatever it was. But by then, he knew. He untied the twine from around the burlap bag, and pulled out the cat. He watched his son's eyes express surprise, then confusion, then sadness.

"Dad," the boy said, "who would do such a thing?"

"Son," replied his father, gently holding the shivering cat, "I'm afraid there are some pretty bad people in this world."

Nate reached out for the animal that seemed eager to go to him. "Can we keep it?" he asked excitedly.

"Now . . . Nate," Jim said slowly, "you seem to forget we already *have* a pet."

"Oh, *please?*" Nate pleaded, stroking the cat that was now nuzzling his neck.

"Well . . ." Jim said, waffling. He could deny his son nothing. "Okay. But I don't think Rover will like it."

"Yes!" Nate exclaimed, raising one small fist in the air. "You won't be sorry, you'll see!"

Then the boy smiled at the cat and petted its head. "Anyhow," he added, "ol' Rover won't live forever!"

That Damn Cat

The Silver Sorrel Somali walked in the gutter along Pennsylvania Avenue, its bushy red fox-like tail dragging in the dirt, a miniature street-sweeper.

Suddenly the cat stopped, and jumped up on the low wall separating the street from the sidewalk. To the cat, the three-foot high reinforced concrete barrier was just another wall—that it was erected after two hundred and forty Marines died in Beirut when a dynamite-laden pickup truck smashed into their barracks was beyond its comprehension, highly intelligent though the Somali was. The obstacle was meant to protect the north end of the White House from a similarly explosive fate—not to keep out a cat.

The Somali crept along the wall, its graceful, elongated body moving lithely, then it jumped down and padded across the wide sidewalk, which was free from tourists and protesters in the early morning hour on this unseasonably cool summer's day.

Carefully, cautiously, the animal approached the black wrought-iron fence embedded into more concrete, and stuck its head through the spear-like rods. With almond-shaped eyes the cat gazed out across the expansive, immaculate White House lawn. Dew sparkled on the grass like millions of diamonds thrown carelessly out onto endless bolts of green velvet.

Quick as the rising deficit, the cat shot upward, over the concrete base and through the fence.

65

With powerful legs, summoning athletic ability account-able to its Abyssinian ancestry, the Somali darted across the lawn, oblivious to any pressure sensors or motion detectors it might be setting off.

From around the northwest corner of the White House, two burly men in dark suits and sunglasses came running, machine guns in hand.

Immediately the cat saw them and froze, a life-like lawn ornament.

The two men fanned out and approached the animal from opposite ends, their machine guns pointed at it.

The cat didn't move.

"Nice kitty kitty," one said. He was smiling, but the smile was nasty.

"Come to poppa," the other one said. He had an ugly scar on his cheek. Under his breath, he murmured, "Fifteen years with the Secret Service, and I wind up chasing a damn cat off the lawn. . . ."

As the two men dove to capture the animal, it shot out be-tween them, and they cracked their heads together in a bone-crunching effect. With a Chaplin-esque pratfall, the man with the scar keeled over, knocked out cold. But not be-fore his machine gun went RAT-A-TAT-TAT, across the other man's foot.

The wounded agent howled and grabbed that foot and joined his partner on the grass, writhing in pain.

The cat seemed unaware of all this, however, continuing its forward assault on the White House.

Now another Secret Serviceman appeared—a bigger and even meaner-looking man. He had a snarling canine on a leash—the vicious dog, mouth peeled back showing sharp teeth, pulled the man along as it ran toward the cat.

Once more the animal stopped. Calmly the feline sat on its

hindquarters, and waited for the dog to draw near.

When the yapping canine had almost reached it, the cat took off, circling around the man, one, two, three times. The dog followed, and in a matter of seconds the cursing Secret Serviceman found himself tied up in the dog's heavy chain.

The cat, a comet now leaving its orbit, blazed out again for the White House.

The dog, too stupid to know what had happened, tried to continue the chase, even though his master called out, "Heel!"

And the Secret Serviceman, legs bound by the leash, hit the lawn with a *whump!*

"Somebody get that damn cat!" the fallen man hollered.

But the Silver Sorrel Somali had already reached the north portico, and was triumphantly climbing the White House steps.

Up on the portico, the cat turned its head and looked back casually at the shambles it had left behind.

It almost seemed to smile.

"Cut!" yelled Christopher Hughes, a wide grin splitting his bushily bearded face. "Fan-tastic!" To himself he muttered, "If only every actor could hit his mark like that damn cat."

The slightly overweight director in grey sweats and baseball cap looked like he belonged at a Redskins game, not standing behind a movie camera.

Out on the lawn the actors began to pick themselves up, joking and laughing. A skinny, thinning-haired young man wearing jeans and a navy windbreaker was ascending the White House steps where the cat sat waiting patiently. This rather anemic-looking man had a silver cat-carrier, into which the animal placidly allowed itself to be placed.

Christopher Hughes turned to the assistant director, a

pretty, bespectacled dark-haired woman wearing a white silk blouse and short black skirt. She was holding a clipboard.

"That's a wrap," he said to her, pleased. "Tell everyone we'll see them back in L.A. on Monday."

"Right," she responded, then hesitated, "For the Oval Office scene . . . ?"

"No, the state dinner scene," he answered, faintly irritated. "Keep up with the changes, Lisa, and for God's sake make sure all those pies are delivered and kept refrigerated. I want to do it in one take . . . otherwise, it's gonna be one hell of a mess to clean up for a re-take."

"I thought the prop master recommended shaving-cream pies. . . ."

"I don't give a damn what he recommended. I told you three days ago I wanted *real* pies. We're in the business of selling *believable* lies—got it?"

"Got it," she said, nodding, making notes.

A Secret Service agent approached them—a real one. He looked no less mean than the actors had.

"Finished?" the agent asked the director.

Hughes nodded. "We're outa here," he smiled at the man. "And again, please convey our thanks, and the studio's, to the President for allowing us to shoot here this morning."

The agent frowned. "Frankly, we advised him against it," he said, "but he's such a big fan of your movies. . . ." He'd said it like he couldn't for the life of him understand why.

"I bet he's screened *That Damn Cat Goes to Vegas* a dozen times," the agent continued. "We have a theater here, you know." He nodded toward the White House.

"Ah!" Hughes said. "Then, please, tell the President I'll send him his own personal print of *That Damn Cat Goes to Washington*, as soon as its edited. Sixteen or thirty-five?"

The agent cocked his head, apparently confused. "Pardon?"

"Sixteen- or thirty-five millimeter? I'll need to know what kind of print to have made up."

"Uh, I'll have to find out, sir."

"Well, do it quickly, if you would, and tell that young woman over there." He pointed to Lisa.

The agent nodded, and stepped closer. He took off his sunglasses; his eyes were tiny black marbles.

"It's too bad someone didn't tell you," he said, lowering his voice.

"Tell us what?" Hughes raised his eyebrows.

"Secret Service doesn't carry machine guns. Unless we're in a presidential motorcade, that is."

"Really?"

"Really. And," the agent continued in a hushed voice, "*we* don't patrol the grounds. The Uniformed Division does. They're more like regular cops." He paused, then added, "But we do use canines, you got that part right."

Hughes smiled at the man. "Well, thanks for the info," he said, "but we knew all that. But seeing some poor cop get shot in the foot with a pistol can't compare to some pompous jerk in shades and a suit getting his toes blown off with an UZI. Now *that* will make the kiddies laugh." Hughes reached out and patted the taken-aback agent on the arm. "That's entertainment!"

Not far from Pennsylvania Avenue, north of the Capitol Building, Todd and Julie sat on the white leather overstuffed couch in the deco-modern living room of their charming little brick townhouse.

Outside, dusk had settled in.

Todd was a darkly handsome man in his early thirties,

with slicked-back Valentino hair, and sensuous eyes surrounded by long thick lashes. His lips were pressed against
the rim of a crystal goblet as he sipped red wine—Chateau
Latour. The jacket of his tan Armani suit lay neatly folded on
the back of the sofa, next to him.

Julie was a beautiful blonde so buxom she approached a
parody of pulchritude, though she by no means looked cheap
in her red Kamali suit. A handsome thirty, but looking it, she
was slouched down on the couch, her shapely legs up on a
glass coffee table, where arts books of Dali, Rousseau and
Parrish lay carefully arranged. Her red-painted, pedicured
toes shown through sheer nylons. Delicate fingers clutched
her nearly empty wine glass, resting it on her stomach as she
stared into the fireplace, its flames dancing a hot little
number.

Todd stared at the orange glow, too, knowing how badly
they needed money, knowing that—in the short-term—Julie
was the one who could get it for them. But bringing up the
subject would be . . . difficult.

"What are we going to do about the car payment?" she
asked.

He almost smiled, but repressed it; she'd opened the door.
Good. Now he had a chance. . . .

"Don't sweat the small stuff," he answered. "First pri-
ority, babe, is the mortgage."

She frowned. "But I'll *die* if we lose the BMW!" she
moaned, then brightened. "There's always plastic. . . ."

He shook his head. "Maxed out."

She sat up, dropping her feet off the table, and turned to
him, looking at him with an expression that was part pout, part
scowl. "You just *had* to have that Rolex!" she said sharply.

He said nothing. He was looking at the painting on the
wall above the fireplace.

That would get her going, he thought.

"I suppose we could sell the Nagel," he sighed.

The strikingly beautiful nude blonde, hugging her long legs, stared accusingly back at them. The modern pin-up in its sleek black-and-grey frame had bold lines, bold colors; a modern, sophisticated symbol of the now distant '80s.

"No!" Julie said. "She looks too much like me. It would be like selling myself!"

He raised an eyebrow. "Sorry," he said. "I should have thought of that."

But, of course, he had.

She crossed her arms on generous breasts and huffed, "Besides, we'd never be able to afford another one."

They sat in brooding silence. Flames hissed on the fake logs in the fireplace. He waited for her to take the conversation another step. . . .

Then she lowered her voice, as if the place might be bugged. "I don't dare 'borrow' any more money from the inactive accounts. Those bank examiners could show up any time. . . ."

"And," he added in a hushed tone, "I can't 'shift' any further funds at the brokerage. Not now. Not again."

"Damn! Is there *anything* we can do?"

They fell silent again. Then he turned and gazed meaningfully into her eyes.

They went wide. "Oh, no!" she said. "Not *that.*"

He leaned close to her, pressing his body against hers. "Just this one more time, to tide us over," he pleaded. "Until I can think of something *big*, to really get us back on our feet."

"But I *hate* it!"

"Nobody's asking you to sleep with anybody, babe. Just a little powder in a cocktail, some sexist letch takes a little nap, and you take his money." He said this casually, as if describing shopping for a specific flavored coffee.

"But you *promised* me I wouldn't ever have to do that again!"

He pulled away from her. "You're right," he said, shaking his head as if ashamed of himself. "I did. Tell you what . . . I ran into that senator's wife the other day . . . the one that couldn't keep her hands off me at the Crawford party? She made it perfectly clear she'd be willing to pay for my . . . company."

Julie glared at him; flames now danced in her eyes. "All right, all right!" she snapped. "I'll do it, damnit! But this is the last time! I mean it, Todd."

He put an arm around her. "Sure, babe," he said, nuzzling her soft, perfumed neck. "I just want you to have nice things."

And he kissed her, passionately enough, but when the kiss had ended Julie pulled away.

"Not now," she said, obviously punishing him. "I have to go get us some money, remember?"

She rose from the couch and picked up her red shoes and padded off across the white carpet toward the bedroom.

Todd smiled to himself and poured himself another drink, and sat back on the couch. That hadn't been so tough. . . .

After a few minutes, Julie came back, her blonde hair hidden beneath a lovely, flowing black wig. She was wearing a tight, low-cut black designer dress, dark nylons and black patent-leather heels; a white fur wrap caressed her bare shoulders. With her white skin and full red lips, she looked like a twentieth-century vampire about to crash an inaugural ball.

Julie extended one hand and jingled her car keys.

"Drive me," she said. "I don't want to leave the car on the street."

He felt a little woozy; he didn't know if it was the wine, or this suddenly incredibly beautiful wife of his.

They went out into the cool summer evening, to the silver BMW convertible parked in the driveway. He opened the door for her.

"Got the powder?" he whispered.

She nodded, and slid inside.

He went around to the driver's side and got behind the wheel. "To the Watergate?" he asked.

"No," she answered, eyes focused straight ahead. "I can't go back there—not after the last one almost died on us. Make it One Washington Circle. And put the top down. I need some air."

He backed out into the street, then followed it to Pennsylvania Avenue, which was pulsing with traffic. They drove in silence. The scent of her Chanel No. 9, borne by the wind, teased his nostrils.

A few blocks from the posh hotel, Todd pulled into a loading zone. Julie started to get out.

"Be careful," he said, leaning over, grabbing her hand.

"I will," she whispered. "I'll call you when it's safe to pick me up."

"I love you," he said, as earnestly as he could.

She didn't answer for a moment. Then, sadly, said, "I love you, too."

He watched her for a few moments, as she walked toward the hotel. Then he pulled away from the curb, and drove back to the townhouse.

Inside, he finished off the wine, then stretched out on the couch to wait for Julie to call.

He hoped she'd come through. Otherwise, he'd have to dump her.

The thought gave him no pleasure: it wasn't as if he'd be

leaving her for a younger woman. To continue living in the fashion he craved and deserved, a wealthy widow would be his ticket. Unfortunately.

Feeling a chill, he rose to turn up the flame on the gas fire, sat near it, huddled there, waiting for the phone to ring.

At first, entering the hotel lounge, she thought she was out of luck: everywhere she looked, in the dimly lighted bar, were couples. Except for one man, sitting on a bar stool, and he looked like a bum! Bearded, in sweats and a baseball cap, he was hardly the sort of prospect she was after.

She decided to play a waiting game, taking a small round table-for-one against a mirrored wall. Somebody would wander in, looking for a little singles action. Some married man, perhaps. . . .

An attractive black waitress in a frilly white blouse and black skirt brought Julie the 7-Up with a cherry she'd ordered. Julie had already had enough wine; she needed to keep a clear head.

"Letting the riff-raff in?" Julie asked the waitress smirkily.

"Him? He's hardly riff-raff, miss. That's Chris Hughes."

Julie sat up straight. "The movie director?"

"That's right."

The waitress smiled, shook her head and wandered off.

Julie took her tall glass of soda with her when she took the stool next to Hughes. She didn't look at him. She could feel him looking at her. Crossing her legs, she began to wiggle her right foot, letting her high heel dangle on her toes.

She looked at her watch, sighed, shook her head.

She repeated this action, every thirty seconds or so, for five minutes.

Finally she smiled at Hughes, looking at him as if she realized for the first time that he was there, and said, "I guess I've been stood up."

A smile peeked out of the bushy beard. "Beautiful woman like you? Seems unlikely."

"Washington is full of surprises."

"You're not an actress, are you?"

"Actress? No, why?"

Hughes smiled again, swirled a glass of dark liquid that was probably bourbon. "Just wondering. I get . . . hit on by actresses a lot."

"Why's that?"

"I'm a movie director. Christopher Hughes?"

He extended his hand and she took it. "Sally Davis. I'm a secretary for a lobby group here in town. Would I have ever seen any of your films?"

"You might. *That Damn Cat*, perhaps?"

"That was yours? Well. I have to admit I may be the only person in the United States who *didn't* catch that one."

He laughed. "Believe or not, that's a refreshing answer."

"But I did see the sequel . . . the one about Las Vegas? I loved it when that cat chased Siegfried and Roy's tiger off the stage! That animal is a wonder."

"I'd like a hundred actors like him. What sort of lobbying group do you represent?"

She thought fast. "The A.R.I.—Animal Rights Institute? We're trying to stop animal testing in cosmetics."

She hoped that would work: between Hollywood and *That Damn Cat*, maybe Hughes would be sympathetic to a cause like that.

"Admirable." He leaned in. "But isn't that a fox fur around your lovely shoulders?"

"Fake fur. Uh, that's our point . . . why should a woman bother with the real thing, when the imitation is cruelty-

75

free? And less expensive."

"Good point. But you also seem to be wearing Chanel. I believe *they* use animal testing. . . ."

"It's an off-brand that smells exactly like the real thing. But absolutely *no* animal testing. I could send you a bottle for your wife, or your girl friend . . . ?"

"I don't have either. Have you had supper?"

"Why, no. That's what I was supposed to have, before I was stood up."

"You know," he said, grinning, "there's something you might like to see. Knowing your interest in animal rights."

Soon they were standing at a door on the seventh floor of the hotel. Room 714. The director was knocking.

"Stan? Are you in there?"

No answer.

"I have a key," Hughes said. He was just a little drunk. "Come on. . . ."

He opened the door and they were in a nice room—though not a suite—and on the bed was an unconscious man in his underwear. He was snoring loudly.

"Stan's the best trainer in the business," Hughes said, "but he's got a little problem with the bottle."

"Should we keep our voices down . . . ?"

"Don't bother. You set an atomic bomb off in here and Stan would saw logs right through it. Look at this!"

He was gesturing to a beautiful bushy-tailed fox-like cat who had also been slumbering, but now raised its head to cast bored almond-shaped eyes upon these intruders.

"There's 'that damn cat,' " Hughes said.

She smiled. She bent over to have a better look; the cat cocked its head and purred lazily. "I never met a movie star before. It's amazing, in the one film I saw, the things this cat could do!"

76

"Amazing. Truly amazing. Now . . . may I invite you to my room, for a late-night room-service supper?"

"You certainly may."

She talked him into letting her serve them a cocktail from the elaborate suite's wet bar before he could phone in a room-service order, and he was slipping an arm around her, risking a small peck of kiss when the knock-out powder kicked in.

He dropped to the floor like he was curtains and the rods had broke. She dug into his pocket and found the key to room 714.

The shrill ring of the phone woke Todd. He looked at his Rolex. It was a little past midnight.

"Todd!" It was Julie, out of breath.

"Where are you?" he asked.

"In a hotel room at One Washington Circle." Her voice sounded strange.

"Did it go all right?" he asked.

"Yes!" she said, then, "No! I'll tell you when you get here . . . take an elevator up to the seventh floor."

"What?"

"Just hurry up. I'll be waiting. I've found that 'something big' to get us back on our feet."

The phone clicked in his ear.

He put down the receiver, frowned at it, then smiled, and ran out to the car.

Todd walked casually through the lobby of the hotel—not too fast but not too slow. He didn't want to be noticed. Which was no trick, the lobby being relatively empty this time of night.

He stood at one of the large, bronze elevator doors and

pushed the "UP" button. He patted his pockets, then fished around in them as if looking for his room key, in case anyone at the registration desk was watching, or some security guard in a back room somewhere had picked him up on a monitor.

The elevator door opened and he got on, and pressed the seventh floor button. He faked a yawn—just a tired exec going back to his room after a boring evening with a client. The elevator door swished shut.

But on the seventh floor, when he got off, only long stretches of corridors greeted him. There was no Julie.

He stood there wondering what to do next, when a door opened about four rooms down, and Julie's black-wigged head popped out.

She beckoned to him animatedly with one hand.

Christ, he thought as he hurried along the plush carpeted corridor, what the hell was this all about? Had she gone too far? Was he going to have to look at some dead guy's body?

Todd stepped inside the dimly lit room. Julie shut the door behind him. She looked gleeful, and almost satanic, the way the shadows fell across her pretty face.

Todd shivered, then noticed the man sprawled across the bed. He was wearing ugly boxer shorts.

"Is he *dead?*" Todd whispered.

"Dead drunk's more like it," Julie smirked.

Todd moved toward the bed and looked closer at the man.

"Jeez, babe," he whispered, "you're slipping . . . I can't imagine *this* geek's got much money."

"Never mind him," she said, "*there's* our ticket to paradise."

He followed her gaze to the head of the bed, where between two plump pillows lay a cat.

"What?" he asked, confused. "*That* damn cat?"

"Then you *do* know!"

"Know what?"

"About *That Damn Cat.*"

"What *about* what damn cat?" He raised his voice, irritated with her.

Suddenly the drunken, slumbering man on the bed gave out a quick snort. Todd and Julie froze. But the man returned to his labored breathing.

"Todd," Julie said in a hushed voice, "that damn cat is *That Damn Cat!*"

Somewhere in his head, a light bulb popped on. "The Washington *Post* did a feature on that cat," he said. "And how they were going to get to film at the White House. . . ." He paused and looked the animal, which looked back at him as if understanding what he was saying. "But are you sure that's *the* cat?"

She told him about her encounter with the director.

He smiled, and started to reach for the cat, but quickly pulled back. "Isn't it dangerous?" he asked his wife. "Remember that scene from the second movie when it practically bit that guy's finger off?"

Julie just laughed and bent over to pick up the cat, which went limp in her hands. She held it against her bosom. It purred.

"I think it only responds to the trainer's commands," she said.

They both looked at the drunk, snoring man.

"Then let's get out of here," Todd said, "before he comes to and starts giving some."

Julie tucked the cat beneath her fur jacket.

At the door, Todd stopped. "You know," he told her, "that article said Lloyd's of London insured that cat for a million dollars!"

"Good," Julie said with a wicked little smile, "now we know how much money to ask for!"

Todd and Julie drove back down Pennsylvania Avenue in their convertible, with Todd behind the wheel and Julie next to him. The cat seemed content to be held in her arms, its face peeking out of her coat.

The street was nearly deserted now. Several limos streaked by, windows darkened, hiding some VIP no doubt, and a few cabbies were on the lookout for late-night customers. At a stoplight, Todd turned to Julie. "Maybe I should put the top down," he said.

She shook her head. "That might scare the cat," she replied.

He nodded, studying her; never had she looked so beautiful. Holding a million bucks worth of cat did wonders for her.

"We're going to be so rich!" he grinned.

"We can trade the BMW for a Jaguar."

"And the townhouse for a mansion across the river."

"I love you," he said, meaning it.

"And I love you."

A car horn blared behind them.

"The light's turned green," Julie said.

"My favorite color. . . ."

Todd drove, the wind riffling his hair. He glanced over at Julie again. Her luscious lips were pursed in the sweetest smile . . . but Todd thought the cat looked strange.

Its head stuck further out of her jacket, ears now pointing forward, eyes narrowed to tiny little slits.

Suddenly Julie shrieked as the cat clawed its way out of her coat, and leapt from her arms into the air, flying like some goddamn Super Cat, and disappeared over the side of the car.

Todd slammed on the brakes, tires squealing, and brought the car to a halt.

"There it is!" Julie shouted, pointing, looking back over her shoulder.

Todd could see the cat walking along in the gutter, then springing up on the reinforcement wall and running along it.

By the time Todd got out of the car, the cat had already jumped down from the barrier and was padding across the wide sidewalk, which was free from tourists and protesters in the early morning hour.

"Get it! Get it!" screamed Julie.

But Todd wasn't quick enough, and the cat disappeared through the White House fence.

"You *idiot!*" snapped Julie as she joined him on the sidewalk.

"Me?" he shouted. "If you'd let me put the top down on the car, this never would have happened!"

"Quit wasting time! Go over the fence and get it!"

"Are you *nuts?* I can't go in there!"

"Look!" she said, lowering her voice, pointing out onto the lawn. "It's just sitting there. . . ."

In the dark Todd could see the cat, not too far inside the fence.

"Go!" Julie said between clenched teeth. Then, almost spitting out the words, she said, "Do you want to lose a *million* bucks?"

Cursing, Todd grabbed the iron rods and began hauling himself up. The bars were cold and slippery. And at the top he had trouble getting over, and caught his Armani trousers on one of the sharp spear tips. *Rippppp!* went his expensive pants as he fell to the ground, cursing some more.

From a crouched position on the grass, Todd could see the cat, still sitting motionless. Good, he thought, he hadn't scared it. In the distance the White House looked dark and quiet.

"Hurry up!" Julie said from the other side of the fence.

Todd was rising to stand, when out of the bush stepped a uniformed cop. The officer had a mean, nasty look on his face, and a gun in one hand.

Startled, Todd jumped, then automatically threw his hands in the air.

"You're in a lot of trouble, pal," the cop said, and with his other hand threw the beam of a flashlight in Todd's face.

"Ah . . . look, officer," Todd stammered, squinting from the glare, "I was just trying to get my cat. . . ."

The cop flashed his light across the lawn, catching the animal in a circle of white. It sat almost bored.

"I don't care what your excuse is," the officer said gruffly, "this is restricted property, and you're under arrest."

Julie called out from the fence. "Oh, please!" she said. "Don't arrest him! It's all my fault . . . I made him go in there."

Now the cop shone his light on her.

She had a hold of the fence, like a prisoner behind bars, pleading her innocence.

"The cat belongs to Senator Hartman," she explained convincingly. "We promised to take care of it for him. Please officer, won't you help us? The senator will be so upset if anything happens to his pet."

Todd, hands still in the air, nodded sincerely. The cop seemed to vacillate. "Oh . . . all right," he finally said roughly, and lowered his gun.

"Thank you," Todd said gratefully, putting his hands down, "and I promise you, you'll never see us again."

The cop grunted, and put his gun away in his belt and motioned with his flashlight toward the cat, which still sat.

"Get it," he ordered.

"Can you help me?" Todd asked. "I'm afraid the cat doesn't know me very well."

The officer sighed irritably, but complied.

And the two men approached the animal from opposite sides.

The cat didn't move.

"Nice kitty kitty," the cop said. He was smiling, but the smile was nasty.

"Come to poppa," Todd said, arms outstretched.

As the two men dove to capture the animal, it shot out between them, and they cracked their heads together in a bone-crunching effect. The cop keeled over, knocked out cold. But not before the gun in his belt discharged, sending a bullet flying into Todd's foot.

He howled and grabbed that foot and joined the officer on the grass, writhing in pain.

The cat seemed unaware of all this, however, continuing its forward assault on the White House.

Now another uniformed policeman appeared. He had a snarling canine on a leash, and the vicious dog, mouth peeled back showing sharp teeth, pulled the man along as it ran toward the cat.

Once again, the feline stopped, and waited for the dog to draw near.

When the yapping canine has almost reached it, the cat took off, circling around the man, one, two, three times, and in a matter of seconds the cursing officer found himself tied up the dog's heavy chain.

"Heel!" the cop hollered. But the dog tried to continue the chase, and the officer, legs bound by the leash, hit the lawn with a *whump!*

"Somebody get *that damn cat!*" the fallen man yelled.

But the Silver Sorrel Somali had already reached the north portico, and was triumphantly climbing the White House steps. At the top, it turned its head and looked back casually at the shambles it had left behind.

It almost seemed to smile.

Christopher Hughes sat on the edge of the bed in his hotel suite, still wearing the sweat suit he'd had on the following day. He held a cold washcloth to his forehead.

The director looked over with lidded eyes at the trainer, who sat on the couch nearby. The man, now in T-shirt and jeans, had an ice bag balanced on his head. The director wasn't sure who felt worse, on this morning after.

"I'm surprised at you," said the Secret Serviceman who stood in front of Hughes, looking down his nose at him.

"A big Hollywood director like you," the guy continued with a smirk, "falling for a gag like that. I thought you were a city boy."

Hughes look up at the agent—the one he had called a pompous jerk in shades—and opened his mouth to say something witty and cutting, but the thought never materialized in his still-doped brain, and the director closed his mouth again.

"You're lucky we recovered the cat," the Serviceman said, gesturing to the animal that lay curled next to the trainer on the couch. "It was the President that recognized it . . . woke him up in all the commotion." The agent laughed, "I think that damn cat would have sat on the portico waiting for its next cue until hell froze over!"

Hughes just sighed.

"And," the Secret Serviceman went on, "it didn't take much for that couple to turn on each other—and turn each other in . . . their kind always does."

The agent frowned and stepped closer to Hughes. "Well?" he said. "You don't seem very grateful your cat was recovered. The paper said that cat's worth a million dollars."

Hughes looked up at the agent and smiled slowly. "And here I thought *you* were a city boy. . . ."

"What do you mean?"

"I mean that's Hollywood hype."

"Hype?" the agent asked, confused.

Hughes grinned. "That cat's not insured for a million dollars. And there's not just *one* cat, there's a dozen of the damn things . . . maybe two." The director raised both hands and started checking off fingers. "One that does the cute close-up shots, one that climbs a ladder, another that high-dives into a pool . . . hell," he gestured to the slumbering cat on the sofa, its back rising and falling peacefully, "running berserk on a lawn is all *that* damn cat can do!"

Obeah, My Love

A bitterly cold Chicago wind, carrying a miserable mixture of sleet and snow, swept across Oak Street, making the simple act of walking almost impossible for a few daring pedestrians.

A woman in a brown mink coat struggled along, clutching its huge fur collar against her face as the blizzard spit into it. The gentleman beside her—his checks as red as if he'd been slapped—grabbed desperately at the plaid Burberry scarf that the wind was mischievously unwrapping from around his neck.

Tanya Green watched them from the window of the espresso-art gallery, *Cafe et Art*, that she owned with her husband, Joel. Despite the warm temperature inside, she shivered.

Turning away from the window, she crossed the glossy parquet floor and went behind the white marble espresso bar, where she made herself a quadruple grande whole milk latte with chocolate syrup and extra whipped cream. Then she took the drink to one of the chrome deco tables and sat down. There were no customers in the espresso bar—or the adjoining art gallery, where her husband was working—the storm had seen to that.

She drank the rich, hot beverage, hoping it would lift the malaise that had been steadily, stealthily enveloping her, just like the storm out there was doing to the city. Hoping, too, it would quiet the voices in her head.

But the chocolate and caffeine only made things worse.

"How are you feeling?"

Joel's voice, right in her ear, made her jump.

"Oh, honey," he said, apologetically, "I didn't mean to scare you."

Tanya looked up at her husband, a tall man with sandy hair, dark brown eyes and thick eyelashes any woman would envy. He looked so handsome in his grey Armani suit and that silk tie with a Frank Lloyd Wright design she had given him for their second anniversary.

Joel bent down and kissed her.

"I just can't seem to get warm enough," she complained after his lips left hers.

"I can turn up the heat, if you like."

She shook her head, her shoulder-length red hair moving in gentle arcs around her face. "Then it would be too hot for the customers."

Joel smirked. "What customers?" He pulled out a chair at the small table for two and sat next to her. "I've only had *one* all day . . . A lady who wanted a painting, and she didn't care who by as long as it matched her mauve couch."

Tanya nodded. She knew the type.

"After an hour I suggested she take a picture of the couch and frame *it*," Joel said wryly.

Tanya smiled.

The two fell silent. Outside, the wind rattled the windowpane, trying to get inside.

"Maybe we should say the hell with it, close the store and head for home while we can still get there," Joel suggested.

Tanya didn't respond. She was watching the storm paint abstract designs on the glass with icy fingers.

"Tanya?"

"Huh?"

Joel leaned forward and placed a hand over hers, which had been resting on the table next to the empty coffee mug. His skin was smooth and warm.

"Baby, what's wrong?" he asked softly. "Is it . . . those voices?"

"No!"

"Maybe you should see that psychiatrist again and get some more medication."

"I'm fine!" she snapped, and pulled her hand away. Just the thought of that anti-psychotic drug made her mouth go dry. A wave of nausea spread through her and she felt she might throw up the chocolate coffee, but the moment passed and she composed herself. "I'm *fine*," she repeated, forcing the hostility out of her voice.

Joel had that hurt puppy-dog-with-big-brown-eyes look again. "I'm just trying to help."

Tanya sighed. "I know you are. It's just that. . . ." She started over. "It's just this *damn* weather!"

The truth was she felt if she ever took that medication again she *would* go crazy! Besides making her lethargic and sick, it put a terrible burden on Joel to handle the finances, which was not his forte. And, anyway, the drug never did silence the voices she heard in her head, only blurred the words into gibberish.

Tanya, staring at her hands in her lap, noticed with despair that one of her expensively manicured gold-lacquered nails had broken off. It took every ounce of control she had to keep from bursting into tears.

"Why don't we go on a vacation?" Joel was saying. "Blow this town . . . get away from the weather?"

Tanya looked up from her hands. "Where?"

"Why not Nassau? We had a great time there last year."

"You mean, *you* had a great time."

88

"What? And you didn't? Shopping? Reading? Sunning on the beach?"

"What else could I do while you were off *gambling*."

Joel's eyes flared. "Hey, I paid you back, every cent . . . or am I supposed to keep 'paying' for that for the rest of my life?"

Tanya leaned forward. "I'm sorry, Joel," she said quickly. "I don't want to fight. Please forgive me, I'm just not feeling very well."

He nodded, his lips a thin line.

"Maybe you're right," she said. "We should get away from here. But I don't want to go back to Nassau."

"Well, what about one of the other islands?"

"Like what?"

Joel shrugged. "Grand Bahama. Andros. Eleuthera." He paused. "There's one place I heard had the most beautiful beaches in the entire world. Hardly anyone knows about it to even go there . . . And no gambling casinos." He reached out and ran one finger down her cheek to the corner of her mouth. "We'd practically be by ourselves," he whispered.

Suddenly Tanya's depression lifted. "What's that place called?" she asked excitedly.

"Cat Island."

One hundred and thirty miles southeast of Nassau lay Cat Island, a mere fifty miles long. Some believe the island got its name because the shape of the land looked like a cat sitting on its haunches, ready to pounce. Others insist the name came from Arthur Catt, a notorious pirate and cohort of the infamous Blackbeard, who made the island his favorite hideout in the early seventeen hundreds. But regardless of how it got its name, one thing was certain to Tanya as she re-read the few pages about the island in the guidebook she'd bought: very little was known about mysterious Cat Island.

On board the MV Seahauler that had left Potter's Cay, Nassau, a little over two hours ago, Tanya looked out from the large cabin of the boat across the endless blue-green water. They were gliding through the Exuma Sound and the ocean was glass smooth.

Joel, seated next to her on the wooden bench, was engrossed in one of the news magazines he'd bought back at the airport; there wouldn't be any available on the island, he'd told her.

The cabin of the Seahauler was full—natives of Cat Island returning home after a visit to Nassau for business or pleasure, their bodies a beautiful brown shade, women in bright cotton dresses and scarves, the men wearing more subdued colors. Tanya tried not to stare at these lucky inhabitants of a world she envied. . . .

A murmur passed through the crowd and Tanya saw a thin line appear on the horizon. She watched the thin line grow larger and larger, until she could make out miles of white, sandy beaches ringed with exotic casuarina trees.

"Joel, look!" Tanya said breathlessly.

He followed her gaze. "Beautiful," he smiled.

"We're going to have such a wonderful time!"

"Knock on wood," he said, and tapped the bench with his knuckles.

At New Bight, the most populated of the villages, all the passengers got off, this being the Seahauler's only Cat Island destination.

Joel retrieved their suitcases, and since there was no taxi service, paid two young island boys, who were waiting for just such an opportunity, three Bahamian dollars a piece to carry the suitcases for them.

Down a sandy-dirt road, about a fourth of a mile along the

coast, was Conch Resort, a complex of a dozen rustic cottages built of stone, driftwood and glass nestled among the casuarina trees on the ocean front known as Fernandez Bay.

Tanya waited outside the main office building with the suitcases while Joel checked in. Above her, whipped cream clouds rowed by in a sky as blue as the ocean, while the sun scattered countless diamonds down into the water.

This was Eden, Tanya thought. Not in a very long time had she felt nearly so happy! She listened. The voices in her head were quiet.

Their cottage, not far from the office, was spacious, with ceiling fans, rattan furniture, a private bath, and a small kitchen. To her delight, there was no phone or television. In several corners hung exotic plants.

"Isn't this a dream?" Tanya exclaimed. "It's better than I'd thought."

"Uh-huh." Joel was putting a suitcase on the bed.

She went over and sat on the mattress that bowed with her weight. "What shall we do now?" she asked impishly.

He stood over her, bent and kissed her, pushing her back on the bed.

"I have an idea," he said.

"What's that?" she smiled.

"Let's go exploring."

"What?" That wasn't what she expected—or wanted to hear.

"Let's check out the island."

"But . . . I thought we might, you know, check out the bed."

"There'll be time for that, later," he whispered, his lips caressing her ear. "Tonight."

She sighed. "Let's go exploring. . . ."

He helped her up off the bed.

In New Bight Tanya and Joel found a quaint grocery store with fresh fruit and fish, and a supply store that sold souvenirs (Tanya bought a barrette made of shells), a Catholic Church and the Commissioner's house. That was the extent of the business district of the village.

At the Commissioner's house was a dirt path and a sign pointing the way to Mt. Alvernia. The sign said Mt. Alvernia was the highest point in all of the Bahamas. In the distance, Tanya could see a stone bell tower on top of the mountain rising toward the heavens.

"I wonder what that is?" she mused.

"I dunno," Joel replied. "Why not find out."

And he headed up the path.

Tanya followed. The foliage got thicker.

In a small clearing on the slope, they came upon a stone house with a wooden door and thatched roof. Next to the house was a white stone oven, smoke curling gently out of it. Tanya could smell bread baking inside.

Clinking noises drew her attention to a big silk cotton tree behind the oven, its low, gnarled branches reaching out skeletally toward them. Her mouth fell open in surprise.

Hanging from the limbs were mobiles made of bones, and wind chimes of bottles filled with things that she could not make out from the distance.

"Joel!" she whispered.

He nodded. *"Obeah,"* he explained. "It's kind of like . . . Bahamian voodoo."

Then out the wooden door of the hut came a native woman in a long colorful dress. Her age was somewhere between fifty and sixty, Tanya guessed, hair coarse and grey and tied up with strips of cloth and string. Around her neck were more bones, and feathers and shells. At her feet was a big black cat, a red ribbon tied around its neck.

"Good afternoon," she said with a surprisingly slight island lilt. "On your way to the Hermitage?"

Joel answered. "Yes. Can you tell us something about it?"

The woman walked to the oven, where she bent to check the bread. Then she straightened and turned. The cat positioned itself not far from Tanya, staring at her with its yellow eyes.

"Was built by Father Jerome," the Bahamian woman said. "He lived there. Died there, too."

"Then the monastery's empty?" Joel asked.

The woman nodded.

"Excuse me for asking," Tanya said, "but what's all that stuff in the tree?"

The woman smiled, slyly. "Charms."

"Charms?" Tanya asked.

"To keep evil spirits away." And the woman went back to the oven.

Tanya and Joel thanked her, then continued along the path which grew steeper with every step. Here and there, placed in the undergrowth, were hand carved pictures on wooden plaques. Tanya recognized them as the stations of the cross.

They were nearing the top, the monastery with its tall, stone bell tower looming, when Joel clutched his stomach and doubled over.

Tanya, behind him, rushed to her husband. "What is it?" she asked, concerned.

"Stomach cramps," he said, out of breath.

He straightened up somewhat, supporting himself with his hands on his knees. "I don't think it's going to go away, if you know what I mean."

"Oh, honey . . . We'll turn around."

"No. You go ahead."

"But . . . where are you going?"

He laughed hollowly. "Probably into the woods some-where. I'll see you later at the bottom."

"Well . . ." she started to say, but he was already heading back down the path. " . . . okay."

"I'll just be a few minutes!" she hollered. After all, how in-teresting could a monastery be?

But when she reached the top she stood dumbfounded.

The monastery was tiny, like a child's play house!

She approached the stone structure, built precariously on the edge of a cliff, and stood before the bell tower, its en-trance coming only to her chin. There was no door so she stuck her head inside, then squeezed her body through.

She was able to stand, but barely, the window at the top of the bell tower she had seen while climbing—and had imag-ined took hundreds of steps to reach—was at her eye-level.

She couldn't help laughing. Was this some kind of joke? Designed to startle or amuse? Or could Father Jerome have been that diminutive?

Tanya noticed a small door by her feet. Crouching, she reached for the knob, opened it, and like Alice in Wonder-land, crawled through to the other side.

In the chapel she had to remain on her knees in a sort of enforced posture of prayer; possibly one, maybe two other adults might also have fit inside. The room was dusty and empty. A half-circle window provided light.

Back outside, in the rear of the monastery, Tanya found what appeared to be the living quarters: three rooms each the size of a small closet. She did not enter them.

A few hundred feet from the living quarters, built into the side of the mountain, she discovered a tomb.

The tomb, however, was not child-size. Over the en-trance, where a weather-beaten wooden latticed door hung half off its hinges, was a large cement slab with the inscription, *Blessed Are The Dead Who Die In The Lord.*

She wondered if they had run out of room for the complete verse.

Was there a tiny coffin inside? It would have been easy to slip past the wooden door and enter the tomb—there was evidence others had—but Tanya didn't, whether out of respect or fear, she wasn't certain.

She returned to the bell tower, and stood on the edge of the cliff, gazing one last time at the breathtaking view of the island and the ocean beyond, salty trade winds mussing her hair. She felt oddly at home, like visiting someplace in a dream she'd had.

The voices returned.

Why didn't they leave her alone? What did they want?

"Go away!" she shouted.

And one foot slipped on the cliff's pebbly surface, and she found herself sliding, both hands now clawing at the rock and dirt, trying desperately to hold on. Her slick-bottomed tennis shoes offered no traction and she knew in another moment she'd go tumbling down the mountain.

She shrieked.

A hand reached out, grabbed her arm and pulled her back to safety.

She sat on the edge of the cliff, trembling, too traumatized to speak. She saw a pair of worn sandals, a black burlap robe, a silver cross, then shielding her eyes from the sun setting directly in front of her, she looked at the face: old and world-weary, but with a hint of a once boyish look. He was tall . . . even from where she was sitting . . . and the sun shining behind his head sent rays shooting out of his skull like heavenly spears.

But something was wrong with his eyes. Was he blind? Yet

he was able to see to help her.

The man spoke, his voice low and gravelly. "Be careful," he warned. "The island is beautiful. But remember, even Eden had its serpent."

Tanya stared up at him. *What a strange thing to say,* she thought.

She tried to stand up, but her right ankle ached, and she was afraid to put any weight on it. So she rolled over onto her knees and using her left leg for support, stood.

The priest or monk or whoever he was had vanished. She seemed alone on the mountaintop.

"Hello!" she called toward the miniature monastery. "Who are you?"

No one answered. Not even the voices in her head.

Panic overtook her. She'd been gone a long time; Joel would be worried!

She hurried toward the path that led downward, her ankle seeming better, and carefully but quickly descended.

As she passed the house with the bizarre hanging bottles, the woman—as if waiting for her—stepped out of the doorway, black cat in tow.

"Your husband went back to town," the woman informed her. "He said to tell you he'd see you there."

Tanya approached the woman. "Was he very sick?" she asked anxiously.

The woman raised her eyebrows. "Didn't seem to be."

Tanya, relieved, thanked the woman for giving her the message. Then she asked her curiously, "How small was Father Jerome?"

"Small? Not small. Tall."

"But . . . the monastery. . . ."

"Father Jerome was a very humble man who believed in living that way. He built the monastery to discipline himself."

Tanya wasn't sure she understood.

"He carved the wooden pictures on the path," the woman continued, "and wanted to make more, but couldn't because of his eyes."

"His eyes?"

"Cataracts. Is something wrong?"

"No. No, I have to go."

Tanya, disturbed, left the Bahamian woman and hurried along path toward town, unaware that the black cat was following her.

Niomi Deveaux didn't bother calling the cat back. After all, it wouldn't do any good because the animal was a disobedient creature. Furthermore, as a "witch" it was worthless!

The cat cost her a lot of money—every Bahamian dollar she'd had. She'd bought it in Haiti because—as every *Obeah* practitioner knew—Haiti had the most powerful witches. She wished now she'd gotten the snake, instead. At least snakes didn't eat so much, or demand so much attention.

Niomi went back inside the thatched-roofed hut, which doubled as a small shop. Rice, grits, flour and assorted canned goods were stored in a cupboard to the left. Straight ahead, separating the shop in front from the tiny living quarters behind, was a counter, its top covered with rows of bottles filled with Niomi's own tonics and medicines. Hanging from the ceiling were local bushes and strips of bark, transforming the shop into an indoor jungle.

Niomi passed the counter into the sparse dirt-floored living area and sat in a straw chair which creaked disagreeably with her weight.

She sighed. She couldn't remember when times were harder.

A descendant of slaves brought over from Africa to Cat Island to work on the cotton plantations, she was born with the gift of Necromancy—the art of calling the dead.

As a small child in the 1930s, Niomi could see the spirits sitting in the gnarled branches of the huge silk cotton trees, and wandering listlessly around the Blue Hole, a large marshy pond in the middle of the island. When she grew older, her power grew stronger and a teen-aged Niomi found she could control these "sperrids" and get them to do her bidding. Her favorite was the pirate Arthur Catt, who was always up for some mischief. But one day Catt literally scared someone to death, and Niomi never "called" him after that.

Word of her power spread throughout the islands and Niomi was besieged with clients—and money. For awhile she remained on Cat Island, but soon left her simplistic life and backwards relatives for Nassau, where she lived in luxury at Greycliff, hobnobbing with royalty and rock-stars who stayed there, becoming a sort of occult icon.

If only her powers had extended to the ability to foresee the future, she might not have lost everything: her money, her reputation and eventually the powers themselves. . . .

"Excuse me."

Startled, Niomi glanced toward the counter where the red-haired American woman stood; she was holding Niomi's "witch" in her hands. The cat was affectionately rubbing its head on the woman's breast, something it had never done to Niomi, being coldly indifferent to her.

"He followed me," the woman said, her eyes darting curiously around at this and that.

Niomi rose slowly from the chair because she'd spotted something on the counter in front of the woman that she didn't want her to see. She'd forgotten it was even there. But the mere intensity of her gaze on the object caused the woman's eyes to follow hers.

The red-haired woman dropped the cat to the ground and gasped.

It was too late now for Niomi to do anything but watch the woman's face register bewilderment, then horror.

"Where did you get these . . . these *things?*" the woman demanded. She pointed to the lock of red hair and gold-painted fingernail floating in a small sea of water in a bottle.

Niomi said nothing.

"They *are* mine, aren't they? My hair? My fingernail?"

Niomi nodded.

"But *why?*"

Niomi didn't answer, but instead bent to retrieve a small tin box from a shelf in the back of the counter. She placed the box on the counter top and opened it. Taking out five US hundred-dollar bills, she put them on the counter in front of the woman.

Niomi felt relieved. Relieved to be done with this deception. Relieved to be rid of the money, in spite of how hungry and poor she was . . . because it was the kind of money that had lead to her downfall so many years ago. . . .

The red-haired woman looked with puzzlement at the hundred-dollar bills.

"I don't understand," she said.

"Your husband paid me to put a curse on you," Niomi explained with a shrug.

For a moment the red-haired woman said nothing, as the words soaked in. "He . . . he wanted me *dead?*"

"No, no, no . . . just to lose your mind."

The color drained from the woman's face, she moved slowly behind the counter and sank into the straw chair, eyes staring, haunted, an island sperrid herself.

Then she threw her hands to her face and sobbed into them.

Niomi went to her.

"You don't have to worry," Niomi said softly, touching her shaking shoulder. "I've put no curse on you. And even if I had it would do no good."

The woman looked up from hands streaked with tears. "What do you mean 'it would do no good'?"

Niomi sighed. "I was once well known for my powers . . . the most famous sorceress in all the islands. Now children taunt me and throw rocks at my house."

The red-haired woman sniffled. "What happened?"

Niomi looked down at the woman's puffy-red face. How could she explain that white magic must only be used for good? And to delve in the darkness of black magic was a very dangerous business. Had the American even heard of the Bay Street Boys, the Progressive Liberal Party, and the malicious attempt to return whites to supremacy in the islands twenty years ago? Most likely not. So Niomi said simply, "I did work for the Devil and God took my powers away from me."

No more could Niomi call the beloved sperrids, place a spell, or "work witch" (the cat had proven that). Even the voices in her head were gone.

"How do you manage?" the red-haired woman asked. She was wiping her eyes with a corner of her blouse.

"I sell bush medicine," Niomi explained, "which I learned how to make. And once in a while take money from people who haven't heard I've lost my powers. Like your husband."

"And just exactly what were you going to do to me?"

Niomi shrugged. "I still have a few friends who pretend to be spirits if I need them to . . . but never mind about that."

The red-haired woman smirked humorlessly. "Well, I have to admit, your Father Jerome had me going."

Niomi frowned; she didn't know what the woman was talking about.

The red-haired woman stood. "When did Joel contact you?"

"About a year ago, when I was still living in Nassau."

"A *year* ago?" the woman exclaimed. "He'd been planning this for a *whole year?* Telling me he loved me all the while. . . ."

Niomi thought the woman might cry again, but then her face became a cold expressionless mask.

"That bastard," the woman said. And she moved toward the door of the shop.

"Wait!" Niomi said. "Take the money. . . ."

The red-haired woman stopped and stooped and scooped up the cat, which had never left her side. "Keep it," she said. "I'll take the cat."

"But it doesn't work," Niomi insisted.

The woman smiled nastily. "Joel doesn't know that."

A dozen questions drowned out the chanting in her mind, as Tanya, cat cradled in her arms, hurried along the dirt path toward the village, and Joel.

Had Joel *ever* loved her? Or just her money? Was he planning to commit her to a mental hospital so he would have power of attorney to spend it? Then divorce her after the money was gone?

That sounded like Joel. So calculating, but safe. She would have had more respect for him if he'd just pushed her off the damn cliff!

Dark clouds gathered and the tropical breeze swelled, blowing leaves from the casuarina trees and bending the thorny braceana plants that switched back and forth like dinosaur tails.

By the time she'd reached the cottage, her mood was as black as the sky, and her mounting rage made her body shake.

She yanked open the door and stepped inside.

101

But Joel was not there.

Tanya backed out of the cottage and walked toward the beach with the cat.

Joel was getting up from a large towel, brushing the sand off the bathing suit she'd bought him at Neiman Marcus. He cast his eyes skyward at the advancing storm.

A beautiful island girl—in a skimpy bikini Tanya would never have the guts to wear—was moving away from him, down the shoreline. Tanya had the distinct impression they'd been together.

She repeated the strange incantation in her head—ancient words—and Joel turned to look at her.

It was her intention to frighten him—with the odd words and the cat—after all, *he* was the superstitious one, but to her amazement the animal seemed to responded to the words, jumped out of her arms and ran like a panther, leaping into the air and onto Joel's back, its claws drawing blood.

Joel threw the animal off, but it came back again and he fled to the water and safety. He yelled at Tanya, his face contorted with fear, perhaps he said "Stop it!" or "Help me!", she wasn't sure, because the wind carried his voice away.

In disbelief, Tanya watched as the cat pursued Joel into the ocean, swimming like an otter (could cats *do* that?), driving him further and further out.

A crowd had gathered on the beach under the blackened sky, partly because of the drama in the water, but mostly because the pretty island girl was screaming hysterically.

A heavy-set white female tourist who'd been drawn out of her cottage by the commotion shouted, "Why doesn't someone *do* something!"

" 'Cause he been *witched*," an island man answered her, shaking his head. "Don' mess wid dat. Don' mess wid dat."

It didn't take long before Joel went under; he wasn't a very good swimmer. Hadn't she told him to stick with the lessons at the health club?

Tanya sat down in the soft white sand and waited for the cat, its black head bobbing out on the ocean's surface, making its way back to her. The sky above began to clear.

Others now joined the spectators on the beach. Down by the water's edge was the priest that had warned her on the mountaintop, his head bowed in prayer, hands making the sign of the cross.

Next to the priest stood a craggily handsome man, wearing swashbuckle boots, tattered pants and leather vest. From his waist hung a huge sword. He was laughing, clearly tickled with the chain of events, and he raised one arm and waved at her. But the others on the beach didn't seem to notice him, or the priest, for that matter.

The cat came out of the water, moving lithely, its black fur matted, and settled next to her. The island people gathered around.

Tanya smiled, at peace at last with the voices in her head.

The Night It Rained Cats and Cats

Officer John Steele was sorry to hear the news about Mrs. Strebel, a childhood neighbor of his, having a serious heart attack.

After finishing his rounds for the day, the thirty-five year old policeman with blue eyes and sandy hair drove his squad car to General Hospital to check on the widow's condition. There, a doctor in intensive care told him the old woman was stabilized . . . for the moment . . . but the prognosis was not good. Steele asked if he might see her; the physician said only if he promised not to stay too long.

As he sat in an uncomfortable chair (to assure short visits, he supposed) beside the hospital bed where Mrs. Strebel lay in a drugged sleep, tubes running in and out of her frail body, he smelled a familiar scent, one that even the strong hospital disinfectant couldn't mask.

It was an odor of cats. Cat hair, cat urine, cat feces.

Steele shook his head. The old lady had lived with so many cats for so long that their malodorousness had permeated her every pore, filtrated every follicle . . . And *nothing* could get rid of it.

Not that he minded the smell; it actually brought back fond memories.

John watched the screen of the heart monitor, which seemed to beep weakly, feeling the machine might straight-line any moment. Outside the hospital room, thunder rumbled, signaling an approaching storm.

He thought back to when he first met Mrs. Strebel.

She was a recluse who lived across the street from him when he was growing up on Mulberry Avenue. But her house, unlike the other nice houses on the fashionable through-fare, was nothing more than a hut: crumbling stone steps led up a terrace overgrown with bramble bushes to a ramshackle shanty with sagging porch, hidden among a forest of weed trees.

It was the witch's house where Hansel and Gretel met their demise—or so he thought as a young boy because of a story circulating on the school playground. As it was told to him by one of the big sixth-graders, a friend of a friend of Jimmy Warlow's cousin went into that house selling Boy Scout popcorn, and the kid never came out.

John and his neighborhood pals, Tubby and Wheaty, would dare each other to sneak up those steps and knock on the witch's door, but none of them ever had the nerve. Sometimes, though, they'd throw rocks at her house from the safety of the street.

It was one of those times that John's mother caught him. She scolded him good, and—to his horror—made him go up there and apologize.

As his mom stood across the street with a yardstick in her hand (to remind him what would happen if he didn't), John climbed the crumbling stone steps to the witch's house thinking ten was awfully young to die.

The first thing he noticed when he got to the top of the terrace was that the place stunk to the high heavens. John had never smelled anything like it, which was worse than the time a mouse got squashed inside the inner workings of their recliner when his dad sat down, and they didn't find it for a whole year.

John rapped on the wooden screen door that was halfway

off its hinges, hoping against hope the lady wouldn't be home.

But then the front door creaked open and a pair of beady eyes appeared, and a long, thin nose with a wart on it.

He tried to scream, and opened his mouth but nothing came out. He wanted to turn and run, but his feet seemed glued to the porch.

The door opened wider and he saw more of her: coarse black hair streaked with grey pulled back from a long face with pointed chin . . . She *was* a witch!

"Yes, young man?" the witch asked.

John found his voice. "I . . . I . . . came to . . . to say I'm s . . . sorry for throwing rocks at your house," he stammered.

A tiny smile appeared on her thin lips. "I see," was all she said.

There was a long silence. "Well, that's it," John concluded lamely.

"Why don't you come in?" she invited.

His eyes went wide. "Huh . . . no thanks, I really got to go."

"What's the matter?" she asked slyly. "Don't you want to see what a *witch's* house looks like inside?" She raised her eyebrows. "That *is* what you call me."

"Huh . . . no I don't," he lied.

"Good," she said, opening the door wider. "Then you won't mind coming inside." And she added with a glint in her eye, "You can tell your friends all about it."

As scared as he was, John thought about that. Thought about being redeemed in the eyes of Tubby and Wheaty, in whose presence his mother just humiliated him. They'd be impressed, and he'd be a hero . . . *if* ever came out again, that is.

And if he didn't, it would serve his mother right for sending him up there in the first place!

"Well, okay," he told the witch. "But just for a little while. . . ."

As he stepped inside, the stench became stronger. He looked around the small dark living room, with its bare wooden floor, worn couch, rickety furniture, (there wasn't even a TV!) and wondered how anyone could live there.

Especially with all those cats running around. They were everywhere—dozens and dozens of them—in the corners, on the couch, climbing the tattered curtains. A constant motion of fur.

"Why do you have so many cats?" he blurted.

"Because no one wanted them," she answered, shutting the front door.

"Oh." He wondered what happened to the dead ones.

She turned to face him. "Would you like something to eat?" she asked. "I can make some popcorn."

"No!" he said. "That's okay."

But off she went anyway, disappearing into a back kitchen that he had no desire to see.

John sat down in a caned chair that wobbled with his weight, its seat repaired with duct tape. He looked around the drab room; the only bright color was a small frayed red rug by the front door. That and the magazines next to him on the floor. He reached down, picked one up and looked at the cover of *American Home* magazine which featured the living room of a home that was even nicer than his.

He bent down again and thumbed through the others, which were more home decorating magazines.

Why did she bother to read these? he wondered.

"Here's your popcorn," the woman said, suddenly appearing in front of him with two small bowls.

Suspiciously, he eyed the one she held out to him, then gingerly took it. She crossed the room and sat in a rocking chair, putting her popcorn in her lap. It was then that he noticed a hole in the floor, next to the rocker, a big yawning black thing . . . Big enough to stuff a Boy Scout down.

She was putting a handful of popcorn to her mouth, nodding for him to do the same.

He wondered if he ate just one small kernel, he might have time enough to make it out the front door and down the steps to his mom before succumbing to the poison that was surely on it. If not, the witch would most likely stuff him down that hole, too, covering it up with the rug, and his mother would *never* find him. After all, it took her a whole year to find the smelly mouse.

John slowly chewed the kernel. It tasted all right. He felt all right.

Then something extraordinary happened.

Up out of the hole in the floorboard came a raccoon, startling John, making him spill his popcorn. He'd never seen a raccoon that close, not counting dead ones in the road.

The cats milling and mewing around didn't seem to notice the raccoon, or the raccoon them, for that matter.

"You always know when I have food," the witch cackled to the animal. She held out a plump kernel and the raccoon took it with its front paws.

"Wow," John exclaimed. "He's tame."

"Yes," she said, patting the animal on its brown, furry head.

"What do you call him?"

"Raccoon."

John laughed at that, and the animal looked his way, spotting the spilled popcorn at his feet; it scurried across the floor, long, sharp nails clicking, and greedily began eating the treat.

John stayed a long time, playing with the raccoon, while Mrs. Strebel (that's what she said her name was) told him all about how the animal had gotten its leg hurt and she fixed it and let it live under the house, and how it was "nicer than most people."

After that day, nobody ever threw rocks at Mrs. Strebel's house. He saw to that.

Steele got up from the hospital chair, went over to the elderly woman, bent and kissed her forehead.

Her eyes fluttered open. They looked confused and frightened.

"It's me, Mrs. Strebel," he whispered. "John Steele."

Her eyes softened.

"You're going to be all right," he told her, trying to sound reassuring. "Just rest. And don't worry about the cats. I'll take care of them."

The old woman smiled and sighed and closed her eyes again.

He stood for a moment, listening to the rain beginning to tap-dance across the windowpane, and wondered if he was the only one who had cared enough to see her.

He seemed to recall his mother once telling him that Mrs. Strebel had a daughter, but that the two didn't get along and rarely spoke. Perhaps he should try to contact the daughter, anyway, he thought.

As he walked down the hospital corridor, a middle-aged couple passed him. The man had a face like a bulldog; the woman, coal-black hair.

There was something familiar about the woman's face . . . She looked like a prettier Mrs. Strebel (but then, who didn't?).

He turned around to speak, but the couple was already entering the old lady's hospital room.

Too bad it took a heart attack, he thought, to finally bring the daughter to see her mother. But even a late reconciliation, he reasoned, was better than nothing at all.

Steele exited the hospital into a dark, stormy night whose sky pelted his uniform with raindrops as big as bullets.

Alice Strebel Hurt approached the hospital bed tentatively. She hadn't seen her mother in over twenty years, and it had been at least ten since they last spoke on the phone, an angry conversation that made Alice decide to never have contact with her again.

So it was a shock to see how old the woman was, lying so still in the bed, like she was dead, which wouldn't have made Alice unhappy in the least.

Outside the window lightning lit up the sky. And as Alice stared down at her mother, a familiar odor wafted up, bringing back painful memories.

Her husband, Harold, came up behind her. "Jesus, what stinks?" he asked. Then, "Is she dead yet?"

Alice glanced at the monitor. "Not yet."

He grunted, looked around the small room. "There isn't a TV in here," he complained. "I'm gonna miss the game."

"We'll go soon," she promised.

"Better," he grumbled, throwing his stocky body into the nearby chair. "Christ, this is uncomfortable. Ain't gonna sit here long."

Alice glanced at her husband, buttons on his plaid shirt straining, belly poking through, and felt lucky to have him in this moment of crisis.

Her mother thought he was a drunk. But then, who could really blame him for hitting the bottle when he hadn't been able to find work most of his life? If it weren't for her waitressing job, they wouldn't have anything. They certainly didn't get any help from her mother.

The day Alice turned sixteen, she left home and married

Harold against her mother's wishes; but Alice couldn't stand to be in that horrible house one more minute. Her mother treated those smelly cats (back then there were only four) better than her!

Now there were dozens of them—maybe hundreds, who knew?—living in the house that should be hers, eating up all of her mother's savings, which was what their phone argument had been about.

Alice had tried to interest her mother in keeping the house up (for re-sale value), by giving her subscriptions to home-decorating magazines, but her hint was apparently ignored.

"We're gonna get a pretty penny for that land, anyway," Harold was saying. "I talked to that development company again yesterday, and they want to put in a bunch of expensive condos."

"But we'll hold out for more," Alice told him, still staring down at her mother. "They don't think we know about the plans for a new golf course just behind it."

Harold snorted. "That'll make the land worth even more."

Her mother's eyes fluttered open, startling Alice.

"Mother? It's Alice, your daughter."

The old woman's lips were moving.

"What are you trying to say, Mother?" Alice asked.

Her mother raised one bony IV inserted hand, and pointed to Harold in the chair.

"What?" he asked his wife, irritably.

"I think she wants you to come here, too."

He groaned and stood and joined Alice by the bedside.

The mother gestured for them to come closer. And when they did, leaning their heads toward her face, the old woman whispered, "My will leaves everything to the Humane Society. So you can leave now."

Then she smiled and closed her eyes and the monitor sounded a loud alarm.

A nurse rushed in, pushing the stunned couple aside, calling frantically for assistance.

"What now?" Alice asked her husband out in the hall.

He grabbed her arm, pulling her down the corridor. "We gotta find that will and destroy it, what else?"

"Where the hell would she've hidden it?" Harold asked, throwing one of the davenport cushions, its stuffing ripped out, back on the couch, causing three cats to scatter.

A search of the living room, now upturned, proved fruitless, as had an earlier one of the mother's bedroom.

Alice sighed. "It's just gotta be here . . . it wouldn't be in a bank . . . She didn't believe in them."

"Then where'd she keep her money?"

Alice thought for a moment. "When I lived here, she had an old tin box . . . If we could find that. . . ."

"Hey! There's a hole in the floor," he exclaimed, pointing next to the rocker. "Maybe it's in there. . . ."

Harold went over, kicking a cat out of the way, and fell to his knees with a grunt. Stuck one hand in the hole.

"Anything?" Alice asked, peering over his shoulder.

"Naw, just dirt . . . Wait a second, there *is* something down here."

"What?"

"I'm not sure . . . YYY-EEE-OOO-WWW!"

Harold yanked his hand back, his fingers dripping blood. "I got *bit*," he screamed, scrambling to his feet. He jammed the bleeding appendage between his thighs and jumped up and down, cursing.

When that didn't ease the pain, he ran into the kitchen and thrust the injured hand beneath the sink faucet and turned the cold water on.

"Here," Alice said, handing him a worn dishtowel. "Wrap your hand in this."

"Now I'll need a damn rabies shot."

Lightning lit up the back yard.

"Say," Harold said, looking out the rain-streaked kitchen window. "What's that?"

"What's what?"

"Is that a garage out there?"

"Shed. It's a shed."

"What's in it?"

"I don't know. Tools, I suppose. I haven't been in it since I was a kid."

Harold's fingers stopped throbbing. "I'm going to check it out. You finish looking in the cupboards."

"Okay."

Taking a flashlight he'd brought in from his truck, Harold went out the kitchen door into a rain that pummeled him with tiny fists. He pointed the beam in front of himself as he hurried along a narrow, weed infested, cracked sidewalk that led back to the shed, while thunder growled above him.

There was a rusty lock on the old shed door, but it easily cracked open with a hit from the handle of the flashlight.

Harold stepped inside.

It stunk in there, too; but instead of cat smell, there was a musty odor of dust and mold.

"What a pack-rat," he said disgustedly, shining the beam around, over piles of housekeeping magazines, old glass jars, out-dated tools. "There's nothing here."

Then his flashlight beam, traveling along a shelf on the opposite wall, halted on a rusty tin container.

113

Could this be the old lady's cash box?

Eagerly, Harold grabbed the tin, opened it, and shone the light inside.

There wasn't any cash, but he did find a homeowner's policy, which gave him an interesting idea.

What if the house "accidentally" caught on fire? They'd get more from the insurance claim than they'd get from the sale of the run-down shack.

He could return some night soon and torch the place (with the dumb cats in it), making it look like faulty wiring—which would certainly be believable, considering the shape the house was in.

But he wouldn't tell Alice about his plan. Not that his wife would be against the insurance scam . . . she would love to see the homestead go up in flames . . . but she might use it against him, in the future, after he left her and moved in with Tracy, a blonde he met a few months ago at the Kum and Go convenience store.

Harold dug deeper in the tin box and discovered a dirty business-size envelope with the words, TO WHOM IT MAY CONCERN, scrawled on the outside. He opened it and inside found the homemade last will and testament of Mrs. Edith Strebel. Leaving all of her worldly possessions to the city's Humane Society, with the provision they find homes for her cats.

He snorted. Fat chance that's gonna happen. Hell. Maybe the will wasn't even legal! But no matter, no one would see it anyway.

Returning the envelope to the box, Harold tucked the tin under one arm and ran back out into the stormy night.

Anxious to tell his wife what he'd found, Harold cut across the back yard instead of taking the cement walkway; he could see her through the kitchen window, standing on a chair, still rummaging around in a cupboard . . . And he grinned like the cat that ate the canary.

But his grin collapsed when his feet sank in mud.

Swearing, he pulled his legs out and took two more steps forward, but went even further in the muck. Now he was up to his knees.

What the hell kind of a back yard was this? he wondered. Had the rain turned it to soup?

"Alice!" he shouted. But she continued in her work, up on the chair, checking the cupboards; his voice was apparently drowned out by the thunder.

Then something began to happen that turned Harold's blood cold: beneath his feet he could feel—and hear—a snap, snap, snapping, as if he were standing on a pile of twigs. And with each new snap! he sank further in the mire.

"Alice!" he shouted again, as loud as he could, and this time her head swiveled toward the window. "Alice, hurry up!" he yelled.

By the time she came down off the chair, and was moving toward the back door, Harold was up to his waist.

Now all around him, small, white round objects came popping up to the watery surface, like onions floating in a cauldron. "What in hell . . . ?" Harold wondered, as one appeared in front of him. He reached out with one hand and grabbed it, and two little sockets looked back at him.

He shrieked and dropped the little skull back with the others, which were bobbing in the mire.

Panic set in. "Alice!" he hollered again.

Finally, she was coming out the back door, covering her head from the rain with her hands. "Harold?" she called. "Where are you?"

"Over here! Hurry!"

She squinted through the rain. "Well, my goodness,

115

Harold, what are you doing out there?"

"Taking a mud bath, you idiot! Can't you see I'm stuck? Get me outta here before I drown!"

"Oh, dear," she exclaimed, now realizing the seriousness of the situation. She took a step off the cement, and immediately sank into the soft ground, then retreated back to the sidewalk.

"Get something from inside, you moron," he yelled.

She turned and ran into the house.

It was the last he saw of her. Or anything else, for that matter, as he was sucked below the muddy surface.

John Steele, keeping his promise to look in on the cats, found Alice later that night, sitting on the sidewalk in the rain, staring out at the back yard, where the officer could see the fingers of a human hand peeking out of the gumbo-like ground.

It took the Search and Rescue Team to get poor Harold out, who was clutching a tin box with his other hand.

Also found was the answer to the age-old question John had about where the dead cats went. . . .

With the money from the sale of the property, the Humane Society built a new building on the edge of town; the state-of-the-art facility, which was dedicated to Mrs. Strebel, was large enough to house all her cats, until they found new homes.

Alice Strebel Hurt was also placed in a new home, the psychiatric wing of General Hospital.

Her diagnosis: catatonic.

Aunt Emma's Defense

Emma Pratt sat very still at the front of the courtroom, waiting for the jury to file in with their verdict. Seated next to her at the small oak table-for-two, was her lawyer, Linda Winters, a middle-aged redhead wearing a tight creme colored suit, sans blouse, that Emma thought was a little too revealing; but then, Emma, being seventy-eight, thought most of what women wore today was too blatantly sexy. She herself was dressed most primly, in a long-sleeved wool navy dress with an old brooch pinned at the neck. It was the only nice dress that she had, Emma having given in to the comfort of slacks years ago.

The antiquated courthouse, with its massive oak railings and brass trim, plaster-repaired walls (on which hung faded portraits of long-ago judges) and ceiling fans, hadn't changed one iota since being built almost one hundred years ago, then a jewel in the crown of the small town. Over the years, Emma had been in the courtroom several times before, doing her civic duty as a juror, until her health made it difficult for her to serve. Now she found herself on the other side of the jury box and very soon, some strangers would decide her fate, as she had helped decide the fate of others in the past.

The pebble-glass door to the jury room creaked opened and four men and eight woman—none of whom she knew—filed in toward their chairs. They didn't look at Emma, their eyes cast downward or straight ahead; she didn't know if that was a good sign or bad, or meant nothing at all, so she tried to remain cool. She glanced sideways at her lawyer, who was anything but cool, fanning herself with a yellow legal pad, beads of sweat dotting the woman's porcelain face, which then made Emma nervous and frightened.

The old woman shut her eyes and clasped her gnarled hands tightly together and said a silent prayer . . . something she hadn't done since her late husband Wilbur lay dying on their kitchen floor from a heart attack several years ago.

Then the judge—a black woman in a black robe—said from the bench, "Has the jury reached a verdict?" and Emma wondered what she had done wrong that brought her to this lowly state. . . .

When her doorbell rang, Emma, from her chair by the front window, had parted the white lace curtain and peered out. There was a boy with blond hair standing on the stoop. He was wearing jeans and a navy sweatshirt; one hand held a black satchel. The old woman thought he looked decent enough to get up out of her chair to answer the door. Wilbur, her two-year-old brown Tabby named after her late husband, jumped down from her lap, anticipating her move.

Often, in this quiet, middle-class, Midwestern neighborhood—where one well-kept bungalow looked just like another—children from first grade to high school came calling, selling merchandise for school projects or church charities or civic functions. Sometimes, the stuff they were hawking was pure junk, and Emma didn't buy; but other times, the items were quite nice, and could save the elderly woman a trip to the mall for a gift—like the clown statue she sent her niece as a birthday present last month.

Perhaps the boy was selling some of those delicious bars of chocolate she'd bought before. (The white spots on the candy didn't seem to affect the taste). She'd just had dinner an hour ago and could use a sweet about now.

Emma shuffled slowly—her gout was bothering her that day—in her house slippers toward the front door. Wilbur stayed close beside her, like a third, good leg.

She opened the door and smiled at the boy. Only now she could see that he wasn't so much a boy as a young man of perhaps eighteen or nineteen, with greasy yellow hair and green eyes. If she hadn't been thinking about satisfying her sweet-tooth, she might have noticed that Wilbur, who usually trotted right up and greeted a visitor, was hanging back, uncharacteristically.

"If you're selling chocolate bars, young man," Emma said with a smile, "I'll take one."

He smiled back, showing decayed black teeth, and she almost changed her mind about wanting the sugar, but then remembered that *she* wore dentures.

"Sorry, no chocolate," the young man said.

Emma's smile fell. "Oh . . . oh! So is it time for nuts, then?"

"Yeah—it's time for nuts."

Emma brightened; it seemed a little early to be selling the high school band nuts, they were almost as good as chocolate.

"Why don't you come inside, then," she offered.

And he did, and she closed the front door behind him.

"Well, let's see the selection in your bag," she said, turning to face him in the living room of her small house.

He unzipped the black satchel and withdrew a long kitchen knife.

"Ohhh," Emma said disappointedly. "I've already got a drawer full of those. Have you got any cashews?"

"No, you senile old bat," he said, lips curled back from the black teeth. "I'm robbing you! Get it?" And he waved the knife threateningly in her face.

"Oh, my," Emma exclaimed, eyes wide. She never expected anything like this to happen. Wasn't it bad enough that there was no chocolate or cashews?

Wilbur, who had steadfastly remained by the old woman's feet, arched his back and hissed up at the intruder.

The boy's green eyes darted to the irate cat and then back at Emma. "Gimme all your cash," he demanded shaking the black bag that yawned open. "And don't give me any crap about not having any dough . . . I know you old biddies don't believe in banks."

"I do have some money," Emma admitted. "But it's not a lot."

Actually, it was a bit of money, to Emma anyway—five hundred dollars that she'd saved from her social security checks by pinching pennies—but he could tear the whole house apart and still not find it hidden in the back of the vacuum sweeper.

Suddenly it occurred to Emma that if anything happened to her, nobody else would find it either.

"Well, *get* it," he said, with a little gesture of the knife.

She started to move toward the kitchen, where she hoped a pickle jar of change might satisfy him, when the living room phone rang, making them both jump.

She looked anxiously at the ringing phone and then at the young man.

"That'll be my niece," Emma told him. "She calls me every day after supper . . . If I don't answer, she'll come here to check on me."

What Emma said was true: her niece, Susan, a thirty-nine year old middle school English teacher, had become a surrogate daughter, as the old lady had no children of her own.

The young man stepped close to Emma, the knife pointed under her chin. He smelled like tobacco smoke. "All right," he said through clenched teeth she was thankful she couldn't see, "answer it. But no funny business or I swear it'll be your last conversation."

She nodded numbly, and with a trembling hand picked up the phone receiver.

"Hello?" she said weakly.

"Aunt Emma . . . How are you feeling today?"

"I'm feeling fine . . . Karen."

"It's Susan, Aunt Emma."

"Karen, don't you think I'd recognize my own niece's voice?"

The phone line was silent for a moment.

"Aunt Emma . . . is something wrong?"

"Yes, dear." The old woman said and smiled to herself; her niece was a quick-witted woman. "Stir all the ingredients together."

Another moment of silence.

"Is there someone there with you? It that why you're talking strange?"

"Yes, that's right. Just one. *One* cup of sugar."

"Is this *one* person trying to harm you?"

"Now you've got it, dear. Bake the cake at three hundred degrees for forty minutes."

"Okay, Aunt Emma, do you want me to call the police? Should I call the police? If I should call the police, tell me to let the cake cool before serving."

"Let the cake cool before serving," Emma repeated, then added quickly, "And next time you're over, please fix the vacuum sweeper!" It was the best clue she could give her.

"Stay calm, auntie."

The line went dead. "Good-bye," Emma said and slowly put the receiver back.

She avoided looking at the young man. "The money is in the kitchen," she said. "In the cupboard above the sink."

"Well, let's go see," he said with a wave of the knife.

Slowly, Emma made her way to the back of the house, with Wilbur padding along protectively beside her, and the young man—knife in hand—bringing up the rear.

The kitchen was a small but cozy: a chrome dinette table with two chairs sat beneath the room's only yellow-curtained window; a white stove and refrigerator took up one entire wall. Across from the appliances was a long counter and sink, and above the sink a row of cupboards that had been painted yellow over a blue that still shown through. And in one corner, a door-less closet held a broom and the sweeper and various cleaning supplies.

Emma shuffled over to the sink and opened one of the cabinet doors and brought down the pickle jar. Filled to the rim with change, it was a heavy thing.

"This is all I have in the house," she lied, holding out the container with both hands.

The young man's face turned more vicious. "I don't want any damn shrapnel!" he snapped and knocked the jar out of her hands; it fell to the floor with a crash, glass shards and coins skittering across the linoleum.

The cat, who had been below, screeched and jumped out of the way, up onto the counter next to the sink.

"Where's the green stuff?" the young man demanded, waving the knife. "Get me foldin' money, or I'll cut your damn nose off."

Wilbur, only a few feet away, reacted toward the threat to his master by leaping onto the young man and clawing him with his front paws, startling the boy—and Emma, who had never seen the cat do that before.

The boy's face turned red with rage and he stabbed the cat with the knife, as the animal clung to his chest, making contact, delivering a fatal blow.

122

Emma shrieked. "Wilbur! Oh, no, no! You killed my Wilbur." And, sobbing, she fell to her knees and gathered the now-still animal in her arms.

"For the last time, where's the dough?" he shouted.

Emma didn't answer, holding her precious Wilbur to her bosom, turning the front of her blouse crimson; but her eyes must have gone to the closet where the sweeper was kept, because the young man turned his head that way.

"What was that you said about the vacuum . . ." he asked himself, then threw back his head and laughed. "You old goats think you're soooo smart."

He crossed to the closet and pulled out the sweeper—a Eureka upright—and dragged it to the center of the kitchen floor. Then he got down on his knees and set the knife on the floor and unzipped the back of the vacuum bag.

There, taped to the inside wall, behind the paper dirt bag, he found a clear plastic bag stuffed with twenty-dollar bills.

He held up the bag of bills. "Eureka," he shouted—his last words—as Emma put the knife in the center of his back.

"Has the jury reached a verdict?" the fifty-five year old judge, Eleanor Hardy, was saying.

Linda Winters wiped sweat off her brow and fanned herself with a yellow legal pad. Three months ago she turned fifty and with it received an unwanted birthday present: hot flashes, the intense, blast-furnace-like sensation that made her want to walk around the house naked (no complaints from her husband).

This morning, while dressing for the trial, even the thin silk blouse she put on under her creme suit jacket was more clothing than she could bear . . . so she went without it.

And, if the hot-flashes weren't punishment enough, she'd put on an extra ten pounds . . . Or else the suit she struggled to get into had shrunk at the cleaners.

She hadn't been eating anything different, exercising any less, so what was *that* all about?

She shifted uncomfortably in the uncomfortable wooden chair in the courtroom, feeling the seams of her skirt strain, and hoped her sweating and fanning hadn't been read as nervousness—although she felt plenty nervous—by her client or the District Attorney, a tall thin man with blond hair and mustache, who sat at another small oak table to her right.

Had she completely lost her mind, where the defense of this case was concerned? Did her depleting supply of estrogen deplete her brain cells as well? The strategy she was attempting, she feared, was right in there with the Twinkie Defense for outlandishness.

Linda shook her head, thinking of a long and glittering career that might very well tarnish on this overcast morning, and wondered what brought her to such a reckless state. . . .

"I feel certain that the county attorney would agree to a plea bargain of manslaughter," Linda had told Emma Pratt and her niece, Susan, who had come to see her after the arraignment and bail had been posted. The three of them sat together at one end of a large oval table in the attorney's law office conference room, surrounded by floor to ceiling legal books, except for one wall where a pastel water-color painting of petunias tried to break the austerity of the room.

"And," Linda continued, "with Emma's age and no prior convictions, she would be looking at very little jail time, if any at all."

Emma, seeming frail and lost in a purple polyester pants suit that was a size too big, said nothing, her skin-creped grey eyes beginning to fill with tears.

Susan, however, slammed a fist angrily on the top of the table. "Aunt Emma shouldn't be charged with *anything,*" she spat. "That kid came into her house to rob her, and probably worse! How many times must she be victimized? First by that boy, and now by the law. It's just not fair."

Linda gestured with one hand in a calming manner. "I agree with you one hundred percent. But do you really want to risk a trial with a charge of first-degree murder? Juries can sometimes be a crap shoot. My advice is to take the plea bargain."

The niece turned to the old woman and raised her eyebrows. "Aunt Emma?"

"I'd rather go to trial to clear my good name," her aunt said, her voice cracking a little.

Linda sat back in her chair. "Then we're going to need a strategy," she sighed, "and a lot of luck."

"What do you mean, a lot of luck?" Susan asked, sounding irritated. "We have a good case."

"Do we?" Linda responded, leaning forward. "I have to consider the picture the county attorney is going to paint."

"Which is?" Susan asked.

"A nice young man, going door to door looking for an odd job to do, is invited in to fix a broken vacuum sweeper, and while he's bent over his work, a kitchen knife is slipped between his shoulder blades by a bitter old woman who wants the money he's made."

Emma's hands flew up to her mouth to cover a gasp. Susan's eyes flared. "That's utter nonsense!" the niece said.

Linda smirked humorlessly. "*We* know that, but will a jury? Again, I have to ask, do you want to take that chance?"

Emma gave her niece a worried look, then spoke softly. "One of my neighbors told me the boy *had* been inside their house, fixing an old lamp, and never caused any trouble."

"Probably casing the neighborhood," Linda responded. "You may have been his first victim."

Emma looked down at her hands in her lap. "And as far as the knife goes," she said, "I couldn't prove it wasn't mine . . . I have a drawer full of mismatched ones. . . ."

"And your prints *were* on it," Linda added.

Susan sat up straight. "My call to 911! That should prove something."

"I've heard the recording of it," Linda said flatly. "You thought something was wrong at your aunt's house because she was calling you a different name and giving unsolicited baking tips. The prosecution can write that off . . . forgive me, Emma . . . to your aunt's muddled state of mind."

"Oh, dear," Susan commented.

The room fell silent.

"Well, what about the cat?" Susan persisted. "We *can* prove he killed the cat, can't we?"

Linda shrugged. "Again, Emma's prints were on the knife. The DA will say she did it to cover up. And it's not a crime to kill a cat . . . Not yet, anyway."

Susan sighed. "Well, we have to think of *something*."

Emma spoke softly. "I wouldn't have hurt that boy," she said, "if he hadn't killed my husband, Wilbur."

Linda frowned at the old woman. "You mean your cat Wilbur."

"My cat *was* my husband, Wilbur," Emma told her.

Out of the corner of her eye, Linda saw Susan shake her head at her aunt and purse her lips.

"Look," Linda said sternly, "if there's something you two haven't told me, do it now . . . I don't want to find it out in court."

Susan shifted uncomfortably in her chair. "Only that Aunt Emma believes in reincarnation," she said, her face flushed with embarrassment, "and that the soul of her deceased husband had . . . entered the body of the cat."

Linda swiveling in her chair toward the older woman. "Is that right, Emma?" she asked. "Do you believe the cat was your husband?"

The old woman nodded, and a tear streamed out of one eye, down her wrinkled check to her trembling lower lip.

Linda leaned back in her chair, staring across the room at the wall of law books. Then she smiled and said, "That's it."

"What's it?" Susan asked.

"The strategy we need to get your aunt off."

"You mean you're going to prove that Aunt Emma's cat was really her husband?" Susan asked with astonishment. "What jury would—"

"It's simpler than that," Linda said, and smiled like the cat that ate the canary. "I only have to prove that *Aunt Emma* believed it."

Eleanor Hardy, waiting patiently for the jury foreman to stand with the verdict, looked out from her perch on the bench at Linda Winters, who sat fidgeting in her chair like an elementary school child who had to go to the bathroom.

The defense lawyer's courtroom performance had been less than brilliant, which surprised the judge. Usually the attorney was forceful; her logic concise, but today, even in her closing argument, when she had the jury's complete attention, the attorney seemed listless, rambling and incoherent.

And half-dressed. Couldn't the woman find a blouse to wear with her suit that was a size too small?

And for Christ's sake, Eleanor thought, what was this reincarnation malarkey? Maybe in top form, with the right jury, the lawyer could have pulled it off. But if Eleanor was reading the jury right—and years of experience had taught her as much—Ms. Winters was going to lose her case—and a poor old lady would pay the price behind bars.

Kyle Slack, the kid that was killed, and at eighteen a man in the eyes of the law, was not unknown to Judge Hardy. The punk had been in and out of trouble since grade school: vandalism, petty theft, drunken driving. If ever there was a jail cell waiting for someone, it was Kyle—not Emma Pratt. But then, a judge was supposed to be impartial and not be swayed by someone's past convictions.

Eleanor glanced at the District Attorney, whose confident expression reinforced the judge's thoughts about the jury's decision. Yet the DA's eyes held no delight . . . nor did any of the jurors, who now gazed at him with soulful eyes.

The judge shook her head and wondered how the hell this case had come to such an unjust state. . . .

"We have reached a verdict, your honor," the jury foreman said. "We find the defendant guilty of murder in the second degree."

A middle-aged woman with short brown hair, seated directly behind Emma Pratt (most likely a relative), was the first to cry out. Then the defendant burst into tears, covering her wrinkled face with arthritic hands, and an ashen Linda Winters put one arm comfortingly around her client's slumped shoulders.

Judge Hardy banged her gavel. The courtroom fell silent.

"Sometimes," she said, her voice bordering on anger, "for one reason or another, the judicial system fails. Sometimes a jury—through no fault of their own—is forced to come to what I believe an unjust decision." She paused, then went on. "Only once in my twenty-six years on the bench did I ever over-rule a jury. This will be a second time. Therefore, I use my judicial power to set this case aside."

Murmurs broke out in the courtroom.

"Sentencing for what I feel would be appropriate for this case, will be set for," she thumbed through a calendar in front of her, "two weeks from today."

And Eleanor banged the gavel again. "The jury is dismissed," she announced.

The twelve men and women stood and began to file out, looking more relieved than upset by the unusual turn of events, some smiling, a few sharing a laugh. Even the DA seemed to have a tiny smile tugging at the corners of his mouth beneath his mustache as he gathered up his briefs and papers.

Judge Hardy stood from the bench and looked over the tops of her bifocals at Linda Winters who was hugging an elated Emma Pratt.

"Counselor," she said, "I'd like to see you in my chambers, please."

Behind a pebble-glass door just off the courtroom, Eleanor Hardy—still in her black robe—sat at a marred-up oak desk, pinching the bridge of her nose, her bifocal glasses in one hand.

On the other side of the desk, stood Linda Winters, looking disheveled, face glistening with sweat, like she'd just run a marathon.

Eleanor tossed her bifocals on to the desk.

"I'm not going to preach," she said sternly, "I think you know what an unprofessional job you did. If I hadn't come to the rescue, that old lady would be in a world of hurt."

"Yes, your honor," Linda replied meekly, her head dropping a little. "I don't know what was wrong with me."

"Well, something surely is," she scolded. "And you'd better figure it out before you step back in that courtroom."

Linda pursed her lips, said nothing.

Eleanor studied her a moment. "Premarin," she told her. "That's what I take."

"Pardon?"

"Premarin," the judge repeated. "Estrogen replacement. It'll stop the hot flashes . . . in a flash."

The lawyer's face flushed—from embarrassment or another hot flash, Eleanor wasn't sure.

"Life gets hectic," she continued, softening her tone. "It's easy to neglect ourselves. I do it myself. But as servants of the law, we need to be at our best. Don't you agree?"

"Yes," Linda responded sheepishly. "Yes, I do. I'll . . . I'll get a check-up right away."

"Good," the judge said. Then, dismissively, she put her glasses back on, and turned her attention to the papers on the desk.

"Oh, he's so cute!" Emma said, looking down at the tiny kitten she cradled in her arms. "He looks just like my other cat only smaller!"

"Doesn't he?" Susan agreed. The two women were seated at Emma's kitchen dinette table.

"Where ever did you find him?" the old lady asked.

"I didn't," Susan said. "Linda Winters did. She got him from a farm just outside of town."

Emma tickled the chin of the silver tabby with one bony finger and cooed at it, as if it was a newborn baby.

"She wanted to come along when I brought it over," her niece went on, "but said she had a doctor's appointment."

Emma looked up from the kitten. "Nothing serious, I hope."

"Just a check-up, I guess," Susan answered, then added, "You know, I think she felt bad for botching your case."

"Well, everything turned out fine in the end, since that nice judge found me innocent."

Emma looked closely at the kitten's tiny blank face, its blue eyes yet unfocused. "You don't suppose," she wondered aloud, "that my Wilbur might come back?"

Susan smiled a little. "You never know."

Emma wasn't sure her niece believed in reincarnation, but it didn't matter. She nuzzled the animal with her nose. "Wouldn't *that* be nice," she said.

When Susan had gone, Emma padded over to the kitchen closet and brought out the litter tray and food dish she had stored there that had belonged to her other cat. As she set the items up in the corner for the new kitten to use, the little animal cavorted on the kitchen floor, playing with a quarter it had found over by the sink.

When night fell, Emma took the kitten to bed with her, where it curled up next to the woman's soft bosom, just as her other cat had done.

Later, when the moon had arched across the night sky beaming silver rays in the bedroom window, Emma woke up to find the kitten peering into her face, making throaty growling sounds.

Alarmed, she sat up in bed and turned on the nightstand lamp and looked at the kitten to see what was the matter.

She looked closer at the animal's green eyes. Hadn't they been blue? And what happened to its soft fur which now appeared course and greasy, and yellow instead of brown? Was this the same kitten?

The animal growled again, showing tiny, sharp teeth speckled with black decay.

Emma sat up further in bed and pulled the covers up around her chin. She remained that way, with the light on, afraid to go to sleep.

Cat Got Your Tongue

The warm California breeze played with Kelli's long blonde hair, which shimmered in the brilliant sun like threads of finely spun gold. Stretched out in a lounge chair by the pool—its water sparkling like diamonds, blinding her in spite of the Ray-Ban sunglasses—she looked like a goddess: long sleek curvy legs led to an even more curvaceous body that spilled over and out her bathing suit, as if resenting having to be clothed. Next to her, on a wrought iron table lay fruit, caviar and champagne. Her pouty-pink lips were fixed in a smug, satisfied smile. She was in heaven!

"Oh, pool-boy!" she called out to the muscular, shirtless, sandy-haired man dragging a net across the back end of the swimming pool. "More champagne!" She waved an empty crystal goblet at him.

He ignored her.

So she stretched out even more in the lounge chair, moving seductively, suggestively. "I'll make it worth your while," she said, her tongue lingering on her lips.

Now he came to her, and looked down with mild disgust. Sweat beaded his berry-brown body. "Put the stuff back, Kel. It's time to go."

"Just a little longer, Rick," she pleaded.

"It's *time*, Kel."

She sat up in the chair, swung both legs around, and stomped her feet to the ground. "How am *I* supposed to get a tan?" she whined.

He didn't answer, but stood silently, until she finally got up and picked up the fruit, caviar and champagne, and shuffled off to the house.

"Hurry it up!" he called after her. "They'll be home soon!"

Rick collected his gear, and after a few minutes, Kelli returned, standing before him like a dutiful child.

"Everything put back?" he asked.

"Yes."

"And straightened up?"

"Yes."

"Do I have to check?"

"No."

As he turned away, she made a face and stuck out her tongue.

They left, out the patio's wooden gate, and down a winding cobblestone path that led through the gently sloping garden bursting with flowers.

"Why can't *we* live like this?" she complained.

He grunted, moving along. "Because I work for a pool cleaning company and you're on unemployment."

She sighed. "Life just isn't fair."

"Who said it was?"

They were at the street now, by his truck, a beat-up brown Chevy. He threw his gear into the back, then went around to the passenger side and opened the door for her.

"But this is *America!*" Kelli said, tossing her duffel bag inside. "Don't we have a right to *make* things fair?"

He looked at her funny.

"What?" she asked.

"Are those your sunglasses?"

"Yes, *those* are my sunglasses!" she replied indignantly. Anyway, they were now.

She got in the truck, and, while waiting for him to get in the other side, checked herself out in the visor mirror.

Now her hair looked like a cheap blonde wig, her bathing suit the bargain basement Blue Light Special it was. She glanced down at her legs; they needed a shave. Cinderella, no longer at the palace, had turned back into a peasant!

"Where to?" she asked sullenly, pushing the mirror away.

Rick started the truck. "Samuel Winston's."

"Who the hell is he?" she exclaimed, scrunching up her face unattractively.

Rick didn't bother answering.

"Oh, why can't you clean Tom Cruise's pool or Johnny Depp's or something?"

"I can take you home."

"No." She pouted.

They rumbled off and rode in silence. Then Rick said, somewhat defensively, as he turned off La Brea onto Santa Monica Boulevard, "He's a retired actor."

She perked up a little. "Really?"

"Lives in Beverly Hills."

She perked up a lot. "Oh!" she said.

They rode some more in silence.

"With his wife?" she asked.

Rick looked at her sideways, suspiciously. "No, with his cat," he said.

Kelli smiled and settled back further in the seat. "Isn't that nice," she purred. "I just love cats!"

With her looks, with her brains, Kelli knew she deserved better in life.

The only child of a commercial airline pilot and an elementary school teacher, she had it pretty easy as a kid, at least until the divorce. At Hollywood High, her good looks enabled her to run with a fast crowd; but it was hard to keep up, what with all their cars and money. Most of her friends had gone off to college; Kelli's terrible grades ruled that out.

She almost wished she had studied harder in school and paid more attention. . . .

But what the hell: girls just want to have fun.

"Slow down, Rick!" Kelli said as the truck turned on to Roxbury Drive. She leaned forward intently, peering through the windshield, studying each mansion, every manicured lawn, as they drove by. She would live in a neighborhood like this someday; she just knew it!

The truck pulled into a circular drive.

"Here?" she asked.

Rick nodded and turned off the engine. They got out.

The mansion before them was a sprawling, pink stucco affair, its front mostly obscured by a jungle of foliage and trees that apparently had been left unattended for years. The main entrance didn't look like anybody used it. Kelli frowned, disappointed.

And yet, she thought, this *was* a house in Beverly Hills.

"This way," Rick said, arms loaded with his pool-cleaning gear. Duffel bag slung over her shoulder, she followed him around the side to an iron-scrolled gate.

"Good," Rick said, swinging the gate open.

"What?"

"He remembered to leave it unlocked. I'd hate to have to holler for him till he came and let us in."

Kelli smiled at what lay stretched before her: an Olympic size swimming pool with an elaborate stone waterfall, a huge Jacuzzi nearby, and expensive-looking patio furniture poolside. And all around nestled exotic plants and flowers and trees transforming the area into a tropical paradise. But her smile faded when she noticed the old man slumped in one of

135

the chairs, head bowed, snoring. He had on a white terry-cloth robe. By his sandal-covered feet lay a shaggy black cat.

"That's Mr. Winston?" Kelli whispered to Rick.

He nodded, with just a hint of a smile.

Kelli put her hands on her hips. "Why, he's older than the Hollywood Hills!"

"You just be quiet." Rick approached the old man. "Good afternoon, Mr. Winston," he said loudly.

With a snore the old man jolted awake. He focused on them, momentarily confused.

He was a very old man, Kelli thought—somewhere between sixty and a hundred. His head was bald and pink but for some wisps of white, his eyes narrow-set and an almost pretty blue; his nose was hawk-like, his lips thin and delicate.

"I'm here to clean the pool," Rick said and set some of his gear down.

The old man cleared his throat and sat up straighter in his chair. "Needs it," he said.

Rick gestured to Kelli. "Mr. Winston, this is my friend, Kelli. Is it all right if she stays while I work?"

The old man looked at her. "Of course." He pointed with a thin, bony finger, to a nearby chair. "Have a seat, my dear."

Kelli sat down, crossing her legs.

"Kel, Mr. Winston worked in show business with a lot of famous people," he explained, "like Jack Benny and Houdini and Abbott and Costello. . . ."

"Don't forget Bergen and McCarthy!" the old man said, suddenly irritable. He leaned forward and spat. "Bergen, that fraud—who *couldn't* be a ventriloquist on the radio?"

There was an awkward silence, and Kelli gave Rick a puzzled look.

Then Rick said, "Yes, well . . . I'd better get to work. . . ."

He gathered his things and left them.

Kelli smiled at the old man. "I didn't know Candice Bergen was on the radio," she said.

The old man laughed. And the laugh turned into a cough and he hacked and wheezed.

"Forgive me, my dear," he said when he had caught his breath. "I was referring to Edgar Bergen—her *father*. We were billed together at the Palace."

"The *Palace!*" Kelli said, wide-eyed.

"Ah, you've heard of it?"

"Yes, indeed," she said. She leaned eagerly toward him. "What was the Queen like?"

"Not *Buckingham* Palace," he laughed, and wheezed again. "The Palace Theater in New York. Vaudeville. You're so charming, my dear . . . are you an *actress* by any chance?"

She leaned back in her chair. "I wish!" she said breathlessly.

"Well, don't," he replied gruffly. "They're a sad, sorry lot." He studied her for a moment. "I'm afraid, my dear, you belong on the arm of some wealthy man, or stretched out by a luxurious pool."

"That's what I think!" she said brightly, then clouded. "But I don't have one."

"One what, child? A rich man or pool?"

"Either!"

He smiled, just slightly. He bent down and picked up the cat and settled the creature on his lap. "You're welcome to use my pool anytime, my dear," he said.

"You mean it?"

"Most certainly." He drew the cat's face up to his. "We'd love the company, wouldn't we?" he asked it.

"Meow." Its tail swish-swished.

"How old is your cat?" Kelli asked.

137

Mr. Winston scratched the animal's ear. "Older than you, my dear," he said.

"You must love it."

"Like a child," he whispered, and kissed its head. "But of course, it's no substitute for the real thing."

"You never had any kids?"

"Never married, my dear. Show business is a harsh mistress."

"What was that word you used? Sounded like a town. . . ."

"I don't follow you, child."

"Something-ville."

He smiled; his teeth were white and large and fake.

"Vaudeville! That was a form of theater, my dear. Something like the Ed Sullivan show."

"What show?"

He smiled, shook his head. "You *are* a child. The Palace, which you inquired about, was only one of countless theaters in those days . . . the Colonial, the Hippodrome . . . but the Palace was the greatest vaudeville theatre in America, if not the whole world!"

Kelli couldn't have cared less about any of this, but she wanted to seem interested. "What was vaudeville like, Mr. Winston?"

"One long, exciting roller coaster ride . . . while it lasted. You see, vaudeville died in the late 1930s. A show would open with a minor act like acrobats or jugglers, because the audience was still finding their seats, you see. That's where I began, as an opening act . . . but not for long. . . ."

He was lost in a smile of self-satisfaction.

"You were a big hit, huh, Mr. Winston?"

"Brought the house down, if you'll pardon my immodesty. Before long I was a top-billed act."

Gag me with a spoon, she thought. "That's so cool. What

did you do in your act, Mr. Winston?"

He laughed and shook his head. "What *didn't* I do!" he said.

The old goat sure was full of himself.

"And that's how you got rich and famous, huh?"

His expression changed; it seemed sad, and something else. Bitter?

"I'm afraid I've not been as well remembered, as some of my . . . lesser contemporaries have." His eyes hardened. "Sometimes when a person does *everything* well, he isn't remembered for anything."

"Oh, you shouldn't say that, Mr. Winston. Everybody remembers you!"

That melted the old boy. He leaned forward and patted her hand; his wrinkled flabby flesh gave her the creeps, but she just smiled at him.

"If only I could have had a child like you." He stroked the cat and it purred. "How much richer my life would've been."

"I'm lonely, too. My dad died before I was born."

"Oh . . . my dear. I'm so sorry. . . ."

He seemed genuinely touched by that b.s.

"Can I ask you a favor, Mr. Winston?"

"Anything, child."

"Could I come talk to you again, sometime? You know . . . when Rick comes to clean the pool."

His delicate lips were pressed into a smile; he stroked his cat. "I insist, my dear. I insist."

The sound of Rick clearing his throat announced that he had joined the little group; his body was glistening with sweat. He smiled at Mr. Winston, but his brow was furrowed.

"Almost done," he said.

Mr. Winston nodded and stood up, the animal in his arms; he scratched the cat's neck and it seemed to undulate, liking the attention. "Will you children excuse me? I'm going to put my little girl in the house where's it's cooler."

"Certainly," Kelli smiled, watching him go into the house through the glass door off the patio.

"I know what you're up to," Rick snapped in her ear.

She didn't reply.

"He's old enough to be your *great*-grandfather. And if he's interested in anyone, it'd be *me!*"

"What do you mean?"

"What do you *think*," he smirked. "He's been a bachelor since like forever. Besides, he's no fool—he'd see through you before long."

"And if he didn't, you'd tell him, I suppose?"

"I might. Be satisfied with what you've got."

"You, you mean? A pool boy?"

"I put up with your lying ass, don't I?"

She felt her face flush and tried to think of something to say to that, but before she could, the patio door slid open and the old man stepped out.

Rick and Kelli smiled.

As Mr. Winston approached, Kelli asked, "May I use your bathroom?"

"Certainly, my dear. It's just to the left off the kitchen."

Kelli grabbed her duffel bag and headed for the patio door.

"Don't be long, Kel," said Rick behind her. She could feel his eyes boring into her back.

Inside she hesitated only a moment. She was in a knotty-pine TV room; the knickknacks looked pretty worthless, and the only stuff of value was too big to fit in her bag. She moved on, like a shopper searching bargains out in a department store, moving down a narrow hallway to the kitchen. She stopped and turned back. She plucked a small oil painting of a tiger off the wall and started to drop it into her bag. But she changed her mind and put it back; she wasn't nuts about the frame.

In the kitchen she turned to the right which opened into a large, formal hallway. A wide staircase yawned upward, as she stood in the shadow of an elaborate crystal chandelier. To one side was a closed, heavy, dark-wood door. She didn't have time to go upstairs and track down the old man's pants and go through the pockets, so she tried the door. It wasn't locked.

The room had stupid zebra-striped wallpaper like the rec room at her drunken uncle Bob's; but there were also a lot of plants, potted and hanging, only when she brushed against one, she discovered all of them were plastic, and dusty. *Yuucch,* she thought. A rich old guy like Winston ought to spring for a damn housekeeper.

There was a fireplace with a lion's head over it—unlike the plants, the lion seemed real, its fangs looking fierce. Big life-size dolls or statues or something of other animals were standing on little platforms against the walls, here and there: a monkey, a hyena, a coiled snake. *Ick!* The couch had a cover that looked like a leopard's skin, and the zebra walls were cluttered with photos of people who must have been famous, because they had signed their names on themselves—she recognized one as that old unfunny comedian Bob Hope. Others she didn't know: a spangly cowboy named Roy Rogers, a guy with buggy eyes named Eddie Cantor. In some of the pictures Mr. Winston wore a weird hat that looked like something out of a jungle movie.

"Koo koo!"

The sound made her jump; she turned and saw, among the wall clutter, a cuckoo clock. The little bird sticking its head out said its name a few more times and went back inside.

She sighed with relief; but the relief was quickly replaced with panic. She'd been gone too long! She must find something of value, and soon.

She advanced to a desk almost as cluttered as the walls and switched on the green-shaded lamp and rifled through papers, letters mostly, and a stack of photos of Mr. Winston, younger and in the safari hat. Finding nothing that seemed worth anything, she looked around the room and then she saw it.

The cat!

Sleeping in a dark corner of the room, in a little wicker bed; dead to the world. . . .

Quickly she went for it, duffel bag at the ready, hands outstretched.

"Nice kitty-kitty," she smiled. "You're coming with Kelli. . . ."

"What the hell are you doing?"

A dark shape filled the doorway.

"Nothing!" she said, and the figure stepped into the light. Rick.

"Don't scare me like that," Kelli said crossly.

"You have no business being in here . . . this is Mr. Winston's private collection . . . things from his career."

"Sorry," she said, almost defiantly. "Can I help it if I took a wrong turn?"

"And what were you going to do with that cat?"

"What cat?"

"Come with me—*now!*" Rick growled. "Mr. Winston's an important account, and you're not screwing this up for me!"

"Okay," she said. She glanced back at the cat, who hadn't stirred. How *easy* it would have been. . . .

On the way out she waved at Mr. Winston like a little girl and he smiled at her impishly and waved back the same way.

"Get in the truck," Rick ordered.

"Oh! I forgot something—my new sunglasses!"

"Hurry up, then."

She hadn't forgotten them, of course; she wanted to go back to make sure the gate was left unlatched.

Larry Hackett had been in California only two days, but already he wanted to go home. The vacation—his first to L.A.—was a major disappointment, from the scuzzy streets of Hollywood to the expensive dress shops of Century City, where his wife, Millie, had insisted on going, though she certainly couldn't afford (let alone fit into) the youthful, glamorous clothes.

And their stay in Beverly Hills with his wife's aunt—a live-in housekeeper for some director off on location for the summer—was also a disappointment; not that Beverly Hills wasn't nice, but he felt like a hick putzing along in his Toyota, while Porches and Jaguars honked and zoomed around him on the palm-lined streets.

He supposed he should just make the best of the trip; sit back and look at all the beautiful women—few of whom looked back, and when they did it was as if to say, "Are you kidding? Lose some weight!"

If truth be told the thirty-five year old Larry was just plain homesick. He longed to be back in his office at the computer.

"Tell us, Aunt Katherine," said Millie, pouring some sugar into her coffee, "what famous people live nearby?" The three were seated in the spacious, sunny kitchen, at a round oak table, having a late-morning cup.

"Well, let's see," Millie's aunt said. She was a big woman with a stern face offset by gentle eyes. "Rosemary Clooney has a house just down the street. And Jimmy Stewart."

Millie clasped her hands together. "How thrilling!" she said. "I'd love to meet them."

"We don't intrude on our famous neighbors out here, dear," Aunt Katherine said patiently. "Besides, I'm just hired help, remember."

Millie frowned like a child denied a cookie.

Larry sipped his coffee.

"Well, who's next door in the deco place?" Millie persisted.

"An Arab sheik."

"No kidding?" Millie exclaimed. "I'll bet some wild parties go on over there, don't you, Larry?" She elbowed her husband, trying to draw him into the conversation.

He smiled politely.

"Actually," Aunt Katherine replied, "the sheik is very reserved."

"And who lives on the other side of you, in the pink stucco house?" Millie persisted in her questioning.

Larry rolled his eyes.

"Oh, you probably wouldn't know him," her aunt said. "His name is Samuel Winston."

Now Millie smiled politely, but Larry sat up straight in his chair. "Who did you say?" he asked.

"Samuel Winston," Aunt Katherine repeated.

Larry, eyes wide, turned to his wife, "Do you know who that *is?*" he asked excitedly.

Millie shook her head.

"*You* know! From when we were kids!"

She looked at him blankly.

"Safari Sam!"

Millie continued her vacant stare.

Larry sighed in irritation. "Didn't you ever watch *The Safari Sam and Pooky Show?*"

"Ohhh . . ." Millie said slowly, nodding her head, " . . . now I remember. I didn't like that show. I could never tell which animals were real and which weren't. And that Pooky scared me."

"Why would a puppet scare you?"

"It wasn't a puppet, it was a *real* cat!"

Larry leaned toward her. "How can a *real* cat play the violin?" he asked, then added dramatically, "Remember its eyes? You can always tell by the eyes."

Millie glared at him—she didn't like to be corrected—then asked innocently, "Didn't Safari Sam get his show cancelled because of cruelty to animals?"

Larry's face flushed. "That was just a vicious rumor!" he said. "Safari Sam loved those animals!"

"I know," Millie laughed, "maybe he *tortured* that cat until it played the violin!"

"Very funny. . . ."

"After all," she said, continuing her verbal assault, "I heard he cut out that cat's voice box so he could pretend to talk for it!"

"He did not!" Larry shouted.

"Did too!" Millie shouted.

Aunt Katherine stood up from the table. "Larry! Millie!" she said. "Children, *please!*"

They stopped their bickering.

"Aunt Katherine," Larry said, "could you please introduce me to Mr. Winston? I'm his biggest fan."

"Well . . ."

"I know all about him . . . his career as a comedian, a magician, a ventriloquist. . . ." Larry paused and stared out the window at the pink stucco house. " . . . Samuel Winston was a genius, a great man! He just never got his due. . . ."

Aunt Katherine smiled, but raised a lecturing finger.

"Samuel Winston *is* a great man. He deserves respect—*and* to be allowed his privacy."

Reluctantly, Larry nodded. Millie looked sheepish.

Then Larry said, "You're right, Aunt Katherine. I'm sorry I asked."

But Larry knew he'd be asking again; they were staying all week, and he had time to work on her.

The gate creaked as Kelli swung it open; behind her Rick was shaking. The big chicken.

"I can't believe I let you talk me into this," he whispered.

It *had* taken some doing, particularly after he'd bawled her out about it, in the truck, when they left Winston's earlier that day.

"Jeez, Kel," he had said, the breeze riffling his hair, "if you want a goddamn cat, I'll buy you a goddamn cat!"

"But I want *that* cat!"

"Why?" he said, exasperated. "It's old, it's mangy. . . ."

"It's worth a lot of money," she cut in.

Later, she had explained her plan on the waterbed in their tiny apartment off Melrose. He'd stared at her, shook his head. "You want to *kidnap* that cat and hold it for ransom?"

"I wouldn't do that," she exclaimed, offended, covering her breasts modestly with the silk sheet.

"Then what? I can't wait to hear."

"I want to kidnap the cat and collect a *reward*."

"Oh, swell," Rick jeered, "well, that's different. A reward as in, somehow the cat got out and we found it and took it home, then saw the ad in the paper?"

"Exactly."

He had looked at her dazed, as if struck by a stick; but then his eyes had tightened.

146

"The old man *is* worth a lot of money . . . and it's just a cat."

"Just a cat," she said, stroking him, "just a silly old cat."

The full moon reflected on the shimmering surface of the pool; it was the only light on the patio. The lights in the big pink house were off.

"You got that screwdriver?" she whispered.

Rick, dressed all in black as she was, swallowed and nodded.

But they didn't have to pry the patio door open; it, too, was unlocked. They moved through the house slowly, quietly, and the sound of their footsteps was something even they couldn't detect, let alone some deaf old man.

Soon they stood in the safari room; Kelli turned on the green-shaded desk lamp. The mounted lion's head and the animal shapes and the plastic plants threw distorted shadows.

"It's in the corner," Kelli said.

"You get it. You wanted it."

"It might *scratch* me!"

"It might scratch *me!*"

"Children, don't fight," said Samuel Winston, his voice kindly; but an elephant gun in his hands was pointed right at them. He had plucked if from the gun rack just inside the door.

Kelli jumped behind Rick, who put both hands out in a "stop" motion. "Whoah, Mr. Winston," he said, "don't do anything rash. . . ."

The old man moved closer. "Aren't you children the ones behaving rashly? Trying to steal my little girl away from me? If you needed money, all you had to do was ask!"

"Please, Mr. Winston," Rick pleaded. "Don't call the cops. We were wrong to break in. . . ."

"Very wrong, Rick. I'm disappointed. I thought you were a nice young man . . . and you, Kelli. How very sad."

Kelli didn't know what to say; she'd only been caught stealing twice in her life, and both times she'd wormed her way out—once by crying, and once with sex. Neither seemed applicable here.

"Rick can give you free pool service for a year!" she blurted. "Please don't call the police, Mr. Winston!"

"I have no intention of calling the police," the old man said.

Rick backed up with Kelli clinging to him. Seconds seemed like minutes.

Then the old man lowered the gun. "Don't worry," he said, almost wearily. "I'm not going to shoot you, either."

Rick sighed; Kelli relaxed her grip on him.

The old man turned away from them and put the gun back in its rack. "I know what it's like to live in a town where everyone else seems to have everything."

He faced them.

"The only thing worse is to finally *have* everything, and no one to share it with."

Something in the old man's voice told Kelli she was out of danger; smiling a little, she stepped out from behind Rick.

"That is sad, Mr. Winston. I wish we could make this up to you somehow. . . ."

His pretty blue eyes brightened. "Perhaps you could! How would you like to live here and share in my wealth? To be my son and daughter?"

Rick was stunned. Kelli's smile froze.

"What's the matter?" the old man chuckled. "Cat got your tongue?"

Rick stuttered, "Well, I . . . we. . . ."

But Kelli rushed forward, arms outstretched.

"Daddy!" she cried.

"Koo-koo! Koo-koo!" went the clock, high on the cluttered wall.

"Ah, two o'clock," the old man said. "Shall we discuss this further, over a hot cup of cocoa? Perhaps you could heat some milk for Pooky, my dear."

"Pooky?" Kelli asked.

"That's my little girl's name. My cat you were so interested in. . . ."

And with Kelli on his arm, Winston walked out of the den, patting the girl's hand soothingly, a bewildered Rick trailing behind. Kelli glanced over her shoulder and grinned at him like the Cheshire cat.

The warm California breeze played with Kelli's long blonde hair, which shimmered in the brilliant sun like threads of finely spun gold. Stretched out in a lounge chair by the pool she looked like a goddess in her white bathing suit and Ray-Ban sunglasses. Next to her on a wrought iron table lay fruit, caviar and champagne. Her pouty-pink lips were fixed in a smug, satisfied smile. She was in heaven.

"More champagne, my dear?" asked Samuel Winston who stood next to her in a terry cloth robe worn loosely over swimming trunks.

"Yes, please!"

He filled the empty goblet she held in one hand.

"Another beer, Rick?" Samuel called out.

Rick, in a purple polo shirt, white Bermuda shorts and wrap-around sunglasses, sat a few yards away, beneath the umbrella, a can of Bud Lite by his feet.

"No thanks, Sam . . . haven't finished this one."

Samuel returned to his chair, next to Kelli. He looked at

her, studying her, and frowned. "You'd better put on more sunscreen, my dear," he advised.

"Am I red?"

Samuel nodded.

"Well, I don't feel it . . . Rick! Do I look red?"

"Not that I can see."

Samuel stood up. "Let me get your back for you," he said.

"Would you? I can't do it myself."

Samuel took the tube of sunscreen off her towel and squeezed some out on his hands. He spread it gently on her back. "Does that hurt?" he asked.

"Not a bit."

When Samuel had finished, he wiped his hands on the towel, then he went over to the cat, which lay on the patio in the shade of the umbrella, and picked it up. He went back to his chair, sat and stroked the animal's fur.

"Are you happy?" he asked it.

"Meow." Its tail swish-swished.

"Me, too, Pooky," Samuel said. He peered skyward. "Such a beautiful day. Don't you think?"

"I'll say!" the cat said.

"Oh, *you-hoo!*" came a grating voice from the gate.

Samuel looked sharply toward it. "Hell and damnation!" he said. "It's that woman next door. That housekeeper. And who's that with her?" He squinted to make out the forms. "Twiddle-dee and Twiddle-dum. Don't worry, my pets, I'll get rid of them."

He waved one hand half-heartedly.

The trio pushed through the gate, the housekeeper marching in the lead, the man and woman trailing timidly behind.

Samuel groaned behind his grin. He put down the cat and stood to greet them.

"Ah, madam," he said, "it's so nice to see you."

"I hope we're not interrupting anything," the housekeeper said with silly little laugh.

"Not at all."

"I don't make a habit out of intruding. . . ."

"Think nothing of it."

"But I'd like to introduce you to my niece, Millie, and nephew, Larry—Larry is your biggest fan."

Samuel smiled politely at the two. "It's a pleasure to meet you," he said.

The niece had a blank expression, but the nephew looked like an eager puppy-dog, beads of sweat forming on his brow. The boy rushed forward and grabbed one of Samuel's hands, pumping it vigorously.

"Mr. Winston," he gushed, "you don't know how much *The Safari Sam and Pooky Show* meant to a little kid with asthma in Akron, Ohio!"

Now Samuel smiled genuinely. "Why, thank you," he said, "That's very gratifying."

Suddenly Larry clutched his heart, mouth gasping, eyes bugging.

"Is anything wrong?" Samuel asked, alarmed.

"Pooky!" Larry cried, pointing a wavering finger at the cat that lay a few yards away on the ground. "It's Pooky!"

The pudgy boy/man ran to it, and fell on his knees, palms outspread as if worshiping.

Reverently, he looked up at Samuel. "May I?" he asked.

Samuel nodded.

Gingerly, tenderly, Larry picked up the cat. It lay limp in his hands. "It's so well preserved," he said in awe.

"I did it myself."

"Really!"

"Taxidermy has long been an avocation of mine. Have you

151

ever been out to the Roy Rogers Museum?"

"You didn't do . . . *Trigger!*" Larry gasped.

Samuel merely smiled.

Larry seemed spellbound by Pooky. "There's a place for your hand . . . he's real *and* a puppet! So that's your secret!"

"One of them."

Larry gave his wife a withering look. "I told you he was a genius!"

The plump little wife, however, only looked sickened.

Larry handed the cat back to Samuel. "Could you have Pooky sing the Pooky Song?" he asked.

"I'd rather not," the old man answered.

"Oh, please!" Larry pleaded, his chubby hands pressed together prayer-like.

Samuel sighed. "Well, all right," he said, but irritated.

"And do the Pooky dance . . . ?"

Samuel glared, then nodded, grudgingly.

" . . . while you drink a glass of water?"

"I don't *have* a glass of water!"

"I could get you one," Larry offered.

"No!" Samuel snapped. "Never mind. Just hand me that champagne."

Samuel stuck his hand inside the cat, slung the bottle to his lips and drank it, while Pooky, his legs and tail flapping in a crazy jig, sang in a high-pitched voice.

"I'm Pooky, a little kooky, it's kind of spooky . . ."

Larry, with joy on his face and tears in his eyes, applauded wildly. So did the housekeeper. But the niece stood frozen, horrified.

"That was just like the show," Larry exclaimed.

"Thank you," Samuel said tersely. "Now, if you don't mind, you must go . . . I need my rest."

The housekeeper stepped toward him. "We were just

wondering," she said, "if you could join us for lunch."

"I've just had brunch, thank you."

"Well, what about your guests?" the housekeeper pressed.

"My guests?" Samuel asked, annoyed, frowning. He turned and looked at the lounging Kelli and Rick nearby; the two had their backs to Samuel's unwanted company.

"Oh, I've been rude," Samuel said. "I didn't introduce my son and daughter . . . they're on an extended visit. . . ."

"We'd love to have all three of you for lunch," the stupid woman persisted.

"Well, I'll have to decline," he said, then added with a wicked little smile, "but of course, I shouldn't speak for Kelli and Rick. . . ."

"Oh, I'm not hungry," Rick said.

Though the trio of intruders didn't notice, the lips of Samuel's children didn't move when they spoke, nor did Samuel's—for he was no radio ventriloquist.

"Me neither," Kelli said. "We couldn't possibly eat. We're just stuffed!"

Carry's Cat

The Annex, in Wichita, Kansas, was considered one of the finest saloons in the whole country, second only to the Alcazar in Peoria, Illinois. But most people felt the Annex was more elegant, with its marble floor and black onyx railing and cut-glass decanters filled with various liquors that lined a long beveled Victorian mirror behind the bar. Even the walls were unique, the grey stucco blocks imported from the buildings of the 1893 Chicago World's Fair.

It was on one of those walls that hung the focal point of The Annex: a life-size painting of a nude Cleopatra taking a bath, surrounded by semi-nude Greek and Roman maidens. The picture, in an enormous gilded frame, cost a small fortune, and men came from near and far to ponder its artistic significance.

But none of the opulent (or decadent, according to some citizens of Wichita) decor of the Annex had any effect on Doctor Henry Carlson, who stood at the high polished cherry wood bar and slammed back a shot of whiskey. He was only interested in the effects of the drink, because after twelve hours of attending Mrs. William Moore, he'd delivered a stillborn baby.

Doctor Carlson sighed as the alcohol burned his throat and relaxed his tight neck muscles and began to dull his brain. Then he set the shot-glass down and motioned for the bartender, Edward Parker, to pour him another. Parker, a wiry man with a handle-bar mustache and slick black hair parted in the middle, filled the glass again with the mind-numbing liquid, picked up the money left on the counter, and moved away from the doctor, down the fifty-foot curved bar, to tend to another customer.

Carlson stared at himself in the mirror. Underneath the black Stetson bowler, his brown hair was greying prematurely, and deep lines were beginning to erode a handsome, if boyish, face. The dark twill serge suit and white linen shirt he had on were rumpled and sweat-stained. He looked like an old man, not the young one that he was.

Carlson turned away from the bar and, taking his drink with him, sat at one of the small, round cherry wood tables in the main seating area, where here and there, next to the tables, waist-high brass spittoons also sat, like squat, open-mouthed patrons.

There were a few other customers enjoying a drink in the middle of a cold, January afternoon. Down at the end of the bar three beefy stock-yard workers were having beers, clouding the reality of their lives, liquoring up just enough so they wouldn't go home and beat their wives and children. And at another table two businessmen lingered, left over from a Mystic Order of Brotherhood meeting, deep in whispered conversation. Although alcohol was illegal in Kansas, having been banned from the state in 1880, some twenty years ago, no one paid any attention to the law, from the saloonkeepers to the public to the lawmakers themselves.

An altercation at the bar distracted the doctor from his present languor. An unshaven, shabbily dressed man was trying to order a drink from the bartender. Carlson recognized him as George Johnston, a once wealthy and prominent lawyer in Wichita, before the man became an alcoholic.

"Go on, get out of here," Parker was saying disgustedly to the man. "And don't come back . . . You disgrace my place."

The drunk weaved a little as he stood at the bar, then raised a bony fist and shook it at Parker. "Five years ago I came in here a healthy young man. You have made me what you see now. So give that drink to me and finish your work!"

Parker scowled and reached under the bar and brought out a Colt .38 which he laid with a clunk on the counter. "Leave, you rummy," the bartender ordered Johnston, "or I'll drain the liquor outa ye."

Johnston sneered in Parker's face. "You don't frighten me," he slurred. "I'm going. But I'll be back."

From his table, Carlson watched uncomfortably as the drunken man stumbled to the front door and out into the wintry afternoon. He felt a twinge of guilt for succumbing to the whiskey himself; a doctor shouldn't be drinking in the middle of the day. And certainly if his wife Sarah found out, she'd have his hide; she was vehemently opposed to liquor.

He stood, buttoning his suit coat, when the figure of a woman appeared in the doorway. She was unusually tall—at least six foot—wearing a shiny black alpaca dress that most women only put on for mourning. Her head was large, white hair peeking out from under an old-fashioned black poke bonnet with its black satin ribbons tied under her chin. While it was apparent her age fell between fifty and sixty, her face, with its tiny close-set eyes, small bulbous nose and unpainted full lips, looked like those of a baby's.

Inside Henry's head, a distant bell was ringing; he thought he knew who she was. But because of the mind-numbing whiskey, the bell that was ringing was without a clapper.

A large black cat crawled out from underneath the woman's full floor-length skirt. The animal positioned itself next to her, by the front door, where it sat as if waiting, eyes hooded.

"Men," she said loudly, addressing the customers, "I have

come to save you from a drunkard's fate." Then she turned to the bartender, nodding her head. "How do you do, maker of rummies and widows!"

And before anyone could say, or do, anything, the woman's right hand came from behind her back, holding a hatchet, and she ran to the bar and brought that hatchet down, cracking the beautiful cherry wood counter, while with her other hand she threw a rock at the Victorian beveled mirror shattering it completely. Large shards of glass rained down onto the lovely cut-glass canisters, which in turn broke into thousands of pieces, spilling their contents onto the bartender, who ducked, covering his head with his hands, trying unsuccessfully to avoid the shower of glass and liquor.

The three burly stock-yard workers, shouting "Tarnation!", and "Let's vamoose!", tripped over each other as they scrambled to make an escape out the back door, while the two businessmen from the Mystic Lodge took refuge behind the far end of the bar.

Henry stood frozen where he was, at last recalling the woman's name: Carry Nation. He'd read about her in the Wichita *Journal*, how she'd smashed Dobson's saloon in Medicine Lodge last month and put the owner out of business, then did the same to every other joint in that town. She vowed she wouldn't stop until all of Kansas was really and truly dry.

As Carry continued to run up and down the bar, wreaking havoc on the counter with her hatchet, in through the front door came two more women dressed in black. They were younger than Carry (and much more attractive); one had dark hair and the other was blonde, both wielding hatchets.

Henry dove behind the bar and hid with the other men—not because he was scared, but because the pretty blond woman was his wife, Sarah.

157

"Peace on earth! Good will toward men!" the two women shouted in honor of the new year, joining their leader in the fracas, smashing everything in their path.

Parker popped up from behind the bar and hollered for the women to stop, then ducked back down as a whiskey bottle whizzed past his head and smashed into the wall, spraying him with more glass and liquor.

Then the dark-haired woman named Margaret—who happened to be the mayor's wife—jumped up on a chair and punched a hole in the top of the oil painting with her hatchet, and slid the blade down, cutting poor Cleopatra in half.

All through the ruckus, the big black cat had remained motionless by the front door—except for its yellow eyes which seemed to grow large with delight. It now ran toward the bar and jumped up on the hacked-up counter, and stood rigidly next to the bar taps, hissing.

Carry took the animal's cue, and with her hatchet, cut one of the rubber tubes that carried the beer from the kegs on the floor up to the faucets, and grabbing the severed tube, began spraying it like a water hose, all over the walls and the floor, and the cowering men, and even her two cohorts, who were busy digging out the bungs from the beer kegs, flooding the floor even more.

Meanwhile, the cat, its black fur matted with beer, began greedily lapping up the puddles on the counter.

Parker had had enough. He stood and shook his Colt .38 at Carry. "Stop this destruction or I'll shoot!" he told her angrily.

Carry turned the hose on him.

Parker fired the pistol, but missed Carry and hit the cat which was next to her on the counter; it fell over on its side in the beer.

Carry shrieked with rage and ran, hatchet raised, toward

Parker, who dropped the gun in fear, then turned and tried to flee. But the other men were huddled in the way, and Carry leaped on the bartender's back, as if he were a pony, and the two tumbled onto the rest, Carry somersaulting forward over the heap where she landed on the floor, sitting in a sea of beer, black dress up over white bloomers, black poke hat askew on her head.

Another shot rang out. A Wichita police officer, a big bulldog of a man in a wool navy overcoat, stood in the doorway of the saloon, his weapon pointed at the ceiling.

"What's going on here?" he demanded as he moved toward the group, sloshing through the beer on the floor.

"Officer," Parker said, his voice shaking with emotion, almost near tears, "these women have completely destroyed my place! Arrest them!"

Carry picked herself up off the floor, smoothed out her dress, straightened her bonnet. "Officer," she said and pointed a finger at Parker, "this man is running an illegal hell-hole. He's a maker of drunkards and widows. And he killed my cat! Arrest *him!*"

Doctor Carlson, who remained crouched behind the counter, took advantage of the diversion to crawl on his hands and knees in the muck toward the back door and freedom from discovery.

"Hey, you!" the policeman called out. "Where do you think you're going?"

Carlson froze. Then he stood up slowly and turned around. "Uh . . . nowhere."

His wife gasped. "Henry! What are you doing here?"

Henry, like most men caught in a transgression by a spouse, took the defensive. "What are *you* doing here?" he demanded. It was lame, he knew.

"Henry Carlson," Sarah snapped, hands on her shapely

hips, "you know how I feel about liquor. Just wait until we get home."

"You're not going home, madam," the officer informed her. "You're coming with me, along with your other two friends." He looked at Carry and Margaret.

"On what charge?" Carry asked defiantly.

"Malicious destruction of private property," he snarled.

"You mean 'destruction of malicious property,' don't you?" Carry responded sweetly.

"That's for the judge to decide," the officer growled. And he herded the three beer-soaked women out—Carry looking back forlornly at her dead cat—leaving the men behind, in what was once the finest saloon in the country.

In an upstairs bedroom of his Victorian home on South Main Street, Doctor Henry Carlson got out of his filthy, soggy, beer-stained suit. Then, at a nearby washstand, he poured water from a floral pitcher into a basin and soaped his face and hands and ran a wet cloth through his hair. After putting on a clean white shirt and pair of wool trousers, he went over to a rosewood dresser and withdrew some extra cash from the top drawer, so he could bail Sarah out of the county jail.

He couldn't believe she was mixed up with the likes of that crazy Carry Nation! Although, he thought, that did explain Sarah's strange behavior lately. . . .

Six months ago his wife joined an organization called the Women's Christian Temperance Union, or W.C.T.U, as Sarah always referred to it. He thought it was a bible study group, with nothing more subversive going on than reading modern poetry, or discussing world events. Now it appeared these women got together weekly to discuss a whole lot more. Like wanting to shut down all the saloons in town.

A horrifying thought entered his mind. What if next they wanted the right to vote? Or, heaven forbid, to become doctors themselves? He shuddered and shook his head. With the coming of the new millennium, was the whole world going mad?

It seemed as though Sarah had. Recently, his sweet, docile wife had become very opinionated and bossy. And her dress had become almost immodest—copying the look of those Gibson girls featured in recent *Life* magazines: tight skirts underneath which (ye-gad) her lacy bloomers showed, and form-fitting blouses leaving nothing to the imagination, her long blonde hair pulled loosely on top of her head, as if she'd just tumbled out of bed. Furthermore, he caught her several times dancing the hootchy-kootchy when she thought he wasn't around.

If she wasn't so wonderful in their four-poster bed, life could be very difficult, indeed. But she seemed to sense when his blood was about to boil over, and so she would stand, in those fancy Paris undergarments, beckoning him with a finger, untying the satin ribbons.

Damn her! She knew the effect that had on him. And there was nothing he could do—or even wanted to do—about it. How could she be such a wanton in private, and such a prude in public?

Henry sat on the edge of the four-poster bed. Maybe he should take his time in getting down to the jail. Maybe staying in a cell for a bit would take the spirit out of her and give him the upper hand for awhile. He gazed at the feather pillows and sighed. Or at least until she beckoned him with a finger, and untied the satin ribbons. . . .

Below, a door slammed, startling him. He wondered who it could be. Then he heard Sarah call his name. He ran into the hall and down the banistered staircase.

161

She was in the parlor, on the brocade sofa, looking sad and weary. But even her torn, black dress, beer-matted blonde hair and dirt-smudged face, could not diminish her beauty. He sat next to her, and the pungent smell of an array of liquor was enough to make him give up drinking for good.

"The judge let me and Margaret go," she said, looking down at hands folded primly in her lap. "But Mrs. Nation will have to stand trial next week." Then she added, "The W.C.T.U. posted her bail so she wouldn't have to stay in jail."

Henry sighed. "Sarah, I don't understand how you could get involved with that woman."

She looked at her husband. "I guess I can't believe it myself," she said. "But Mrs. Nation came to our meeting this afternoon and gave such a rousing speech about the evils of liquor . . . Then poor Mrs. McCabe stood up and said her husband went on a toot last week and spent all his pay—and her with four little children to feed—and then Mrs. Johnston said she had to throw her husband out of the house because his drinking made him so violent. . . ." She stopped to catch her breath, and added emphatically, "If men aren't going to obey the anti-liquor law, then women will have to do something about it!"

Henry looked into his wife's tear-filled eyes. "Sarah, you can't fix a law by breaking another. You could have been hurt, or worse."

They fell silent for a moment. Then his wife said softly, "I know why you were there. I heard about the baby. Henry, next time, why don't you turn to me, instead of liquor?"

He smiled just a little. "Don't worry. I saw the way you handled that hatchet."

An urgent pounding at the front door put an end to their conversation. Sarah gestured to her disheveled appearance and jumped up from the sofa and hurried toward the stairs, as Henry headed for the entryway to answer the insistent knocking. But before he could get there, the door opened, and Margaret ran in. She had changed from her black dress into a long green velvet one, her dark hair pulled neatly back into a bun, but her expression was just as wild as when Henry saw her bashing the saloon.

"Something terrible has happened," she wailed, rushing past Henry, to the foot of the stairs where she looked up at Sarah, who had stopped, halfway up.

Sarah turned and came down to her friend. "What is it?"

"Someone found that bar owner, Edward Parker, in the Annex saloon hacked to death with a hatchet," she said. "And they've arrested Carry for it!"

It wasn't the first time Carry Nation had been in jail. Back in Medicine Lodge, she spent two weeks in a cell for destroying Dobson's saloon, not having the money herself for bail. But at the trial, the judge ("Your Dishonor," she snidely called him) let her go for insufficient evidence, even though half the town had witnessed her "hatchetation." Then the Sheriff gave her money and a railway ticket to get out of town, which she did, but she used the money to buy more hatchets and came back and smashed another saloon, and another, until they were all closed down.

But this time was different. She'd never been jailed for murder. With the saloon smashing, no one dared to prosecute her. How could they? They would have to admit that *they* were the ones breaking the law by allowing saloons to flourish. She was only correcting the situation, acting as an enforcer because they would not. But now, with the bartender killed with one of her hatchets, things didn't look so good.

After the nice women from the local Temperance Union paid her bail money for "disturbing the peace," Carry had gone back to her hotel to freshen up and put on a clean black dress before heading over to the ruins of the Annex Saloon to retrieve her dead cat. She and the animal had been through many a saloon smashing together and she felt he deserved a proper burial, not to be thrown out with the rubble.

When she got there, the cat was still lying on the counter in a pool of beer and blood, one of her hatchets next to it. She picked up the hatchet so she wouldn't have to buy another, then went around the counter to find a carton or box to put the cat in, and discovered the chopped-up Parker. Then she rushed out to the street, hatchet still in hand, and ran into the two businessmen who had been drinking in the saloon earlier. They were the ones who told the police she had done the deed.

No, this time the situation did not look so good.

In the cold, grey cell, Carry dropped down off the cot where she'd been sitting and onto her knees. "Oh, Lord," she prayed. "You told me to call on you in my day of trouble. Well Sir, this is my day of trouble!"

Then, head bowed, she advanced on her knees around the small cell, a curious practice taught to her as a small child by the God-fearing slaves on her father's cotton plantation.

With her praying done, she returned to sit on the cot. Her thoughts turned back to the cat.

The animal had been such a comfort to her this past year on her crusade. It was after her second saloon smashing in Medicine Lodge that she noticed the mangy black cat began to appear, watching, waiting, knowing that where Carry went liquor would surely flow.

Some might wonder why a woman opposed to alcohol

would keep an alcoholic cat around, but Carry saw the animal as a reminder that creatures both great and small could be affected by the evils of drink.

And the cat was really quite loving (when sober), snuggling up with her in various hotel rooms, keeping loneliness at bay. Carry, after all, had very little family life. Her ex-husband, Charles, had concealed his drinking during their courtship, then after their marriage came home night after night drunker than a skunk, eventually ruining his medical practice and their personal finances, and finally the marriage itself. Their daughter, Charlien, born retarded, also grew up to become an alcoholic and had to be institutionalized because of her excessive drinking. Often Carry wondered if Charles' addiction had somehow contributed to her bearing a dim-witted child; she remembered the Bible's warning against pregnancy and alcohol.

Softly, Carry began to sing "Am I a Soldier of the Cross?", and after the first verse, a male voice from another cell joined in, and then another, and another, as the sky outside the little cell windows darkened and night moved in.

It was nearly midnight when Henry Carlson entered the back door of the County Morgue, which was in the basement of a clapboard building next to the police station.

He was not the doctor acting as coroner, but knew the man well, and had arranged earlier a chance to see the body of bartender Edward Parker.

The coroner, a small, plump man with a balding head and thick-lens glasses, opened the door to the back and let him in out of the cold.

A gas lamp on the wall cast long dark shadows, making the room seem creepy even to Henry who was used to such things.

"Don't let the chief know about this," the coroner whispered.

"Don't worry," Henry answered.

"He's over here," the coroner said, pointing to the wooden coffin. "You'll want to hold your nose."

Henry had several reasons for wanting a look at Parker's remains. One was when he'd heard the two men from the Mystic Order of Brotherhood had pointed an accusing finger at Mrs. Nation he became suspicious of their motives. He knew that the Brotherhood—apparently, like the women's Temperance Union—was not a benign organization. In fact, The Mystic Order of Brotherhood was really a front for the continuing efforts of the liquor industry. But not everyone knew that.

The second reason he was standing in the morgue in the middle of the night, poking at dismembered body parts, was his wife Sarah, who was completely inconsolable since Mrs. Nation was arrested. She was convinced that Mrs. Nation could not have done such an awful thing, even though the old woman could wield a hatchet with the savagery of an Apache. But if it was one thing Henry couldn't stand, it was his beautiful wife in tears.

"Look there," Henry said to the coroner.

"Where?"

"There."

"I don't see what you mean."

Henry poked some more at the torso. "Where the hatchet went into his heart. Do you see it now?"

The coroner drew in a sharp breath. "My God. Is that . . . a bullet wound?" He looked at Henry. "I'd say this changes everything."

Henry nodded. "I think you'll find that bullet was what killed Parker, and the hacking was done to cover it up and place the blame on Carry Nation."

The coroner's eyes grew larger behind his thick glasses. "You don't think those two men—the witnesses—did this, to frame Mrs. Nation?"

Henry thought for a moment. "I just can't see either of them killing Parker," he said, "but I can see them taking advantage of an already bad situation, if you know what I mean." Then he added, "However, Mrs. Nation certainly has the liquor industry riled, and these are crazy times."

They were moving toward the back door, the coroner turning out the gas light. "Well, if they didn't do it, who besides Carry Nation would want to kill Edward Parker?"

Henry shrugged, then straightened up, half-smiled. "I can think of one."

McNab's Livery was just a short walk from the County Morgue, and Henry hoofed it over there, holding the collar of his wool coat up around his face against the bitter winter night wind, the full moon above watching like a popped out eye.

John McNab was a patient of his and he remembered the stable owner once mentioned he let some of the drunks sleep there when it got so cold.

The barn door creaked as Henry opened it, startling a couple Palominos, who snorted and eyed him wildly, until he shushed them quietly and moved slowly by.

He found George Johnston asleep in the last stall, buried beneath some straw. He knelt down next to the man, who smelled almost as bad as the remains of Edward Parker, the combination of liquor and inhumanity almost unbearable.

Henry gently shook the man, whose eyes opened, frightened as the horses'.

"It's Doc Carlson," Henry said softly. "No need to be afraid."

Johnston sat up, straw falling away from his frayed coat. "Doc," the man said, tongue lolling around in a dry mouth, "have you got any money for a drink?" He held out a dirty hand.

"Sure, George," Henry replied, and dug into his waistcoat pocket, then put a coin into the man's palm. "You go and see Edward Parker tomorrow and he'll give you a drink."

Johnston dropped the coin, like it was a hot coal, and it disappeared into the straw. His eyes looked frightened.

"I think he treated you badly today," Henry said. "When all you wanted was a drink."

Johnston's already rheumy eyes took on a wetter look, his lower lip trembling. "I warned him I'd be back," he said.

"You knew the gun was under the counter and shot him, didn't you, George?" Henry asked softly.

Johnston nodded and lowered his head. "In the heart . . . because he had none."

Henry looked at the once wealthy and prominent lawyer. "You go back to sleep now George," he told the man, and patted his shoulder. The police could pick him up in the morning.

Henry covered up the already slumbering Johnston with straw, before slipping quietly out.

In the parlor of Henry's Victorian home, Carry Nation, wearing her trademark black alpaca dress and black poke bonnet, looking regal as a queen as she sat in a high-back rosewood chair, sipped the tea Sarah has just served. Henry and Sarah were across from her, on the brocade sofa. Flames danced in the fireplace.

"I can't thank you both enough for clearing my good name," Mrs. Nation said.

"It was all Henry's doing," Sarah said, looking gratefully at her husband.

Henry smiled, enjoying the moment of adulation in his wife's blue eyes.

"What do you suppose will happen to the two men who tried to put the blame on Carry?" Sarah asked her husband.

Henry shrugged. "That will be up to the judge to decide. But they did admit to seeing Johnston shoot Parker and flee, and decided to use the hatchet on the poor man to make it seem like Mrs. Nation did the awful deed."

The trio was silent for a moment, then Henry asked Carry, "What are your plans now?"

Carry set her cup and saucer on a small pedestal next to her chair. "I'm off to the Senate in Topeka," she announced.

"Oh," Sarah said brightly, "You're finally going to speak to the legislature."

Mrs. Nation frowned. "No, my dear," she replied, "The Senate *Bar*. It's across from the legislature, and all those Republican rummies hang out there . . . So I'm sure they'll get my message."

She reached inside her black cloth purse on her lap. "I'm financing the trip with these," she told them, pulling out a handful of miniature pewter hatchets. "A company in Rhode Island is making them for me. I'll sell them for ten cents a piece—or twenty five, if I think I can get it."

Henry and Sarah laughed.

Then Carry stood up. "I must be going. My train leaves shortly. Thank you again for all you have done."

"Will you wait just a moment?" Sarah said to Carry. "We have something for you." And Sarah nodded at Henry who left the room.

Soon Henry came back carrying a small black kitten. And when Carry saw the animal her face burst into a smile of joy, and she rushed to it, plucking it out of Henry's hands, and held the furry thing against her face.

"It's not partial to liquor of any kind," Henry told her.

"And I'll see that it never is!" Carry said with tears in her eyes.

After Mrs. Nation left, Henry gathered up the teacups and carried them into the kitchen. When he returned, Sarah had left the room; he could hear her upstairs moving around in the bedroom.

He climbed the staircase smiling to himself; his heroics should garner a lot of favors with his wife. Like staying out all night, playing poker with the boys, or buying that new contraption Henry Ford had just invented. Yes, for a while, he was going to have the upper hand. . . .

He halted in the doorway to the bedroom, where Sarah now stood next to the four-poster bed, in her fancy Paris undergarments, a seductive smile on her face.

. . . or anyway, until his wife beckoned to him with her finger, and untied the satin ribbons.

To Grandmother's House We Go

Lydia May Albright, nine years old, sat in the backseat of her parents' late model Ford Thunderbird as the car traveled along a snowy two-lane highway in northern Minnesota, with her father at the wheel and her mother beside him. The little girl was wearing a new red corduroy dress with a white lace collar, white tights and black patent leather shoes. With her long blond hair, bright blue eyes, tiny button nose and pink cherub mouth, she looked like a china doll come to life. Next to her, on the back seat, slept the family cat, Fluffy, a white Persian, curled up on the girl's red woolen coat. For never having made the long car trip before, the feline was doing quite well.

Lydia looked out the window of the car at the winter-wonderland scenery whizzing by and couldn't remember *ever* feeling happier.

The snow outside that covered the thick pine tree forests was not the heavy kind good for making snowballs or snowmen—it was the kind of snow that crunched under your shoes when you walked, and crumbled apart in your hand if you tried to mold it. *This* snow sparkled, just like the glitter on the front of the Thanksgiving greeting card Lydia held in her hand.

She bought the card yesterday with her mother, at the Hallmark store in the mall, passing over the more modern and mundane greetings of pumpkins and turkeys for this traditional one. Besides the fake snow, the outside of the card showed a family riding in an old-fashioned sleigh—a father, mother, little boy and little girl. While she didn't have a brother, the parents looked a lot like hers, and the little girl seemed a mirror image of herself.

But she hadn't picked the card because of the glitter or the family in the sleigh, or even because of a poem that was printed throughout and written by a person with the same first name as hers . . . She had picked the card because of what was *inside*.

Lydia opened the card. And smiled at the picture of an old Victorian farmhouse—just like the house where they were going—and on the front porch stood a plump old woman in an apron and funny cap, her arms outstretched, a look of joy on her grandmotherly face. . . .

"Are you still fiddling with that card?" her mother asked, glancing back at her daughter. She sounded cross, but Lydia could see a smile tugging at the corners of her ruby-stained mouth. "It'll be in tatters before we get there," she warned.

Lydia thought her mother looked so pretty in her green coat with plaid velvet collar, and shoulder length brown hair gathered at the neck with a green velvet bow. Her make-up was heavier than Lydia had ever seen her mother wear; she could have been a movie star.

And for once her mother didn't have a bad headache.

"What's that, dear?" Lydia's father asked her mother. A middle-aged man with dark hair and a handsome, chiseled face, he was wearing a colorful sweater over a pale polo shirt.

"A card she bought for Grandmother," explained Lydia's mother.

"Oh, yes," he replied, looking at his daughter in the rear view mirror. "I saw it on the dining room table. Very nice, Lydia. It reminds me of Thanksgiving with my grandparents when I was a little kid."

And he began to sing the poem that was printed on the card. "Over the river and through the wood to Grandmother's house we go. . . ."

Lydia beamed. So the poem was a *song,* too! She listened, enraptured, to her father's deep voice. After a minute her mother joined in. She had a nice voice, too. "Oh, how the wind does blow! It stings the toes and bites the nose, as over the ground we go."

Her parents stopped singing and laughed, her father reaching out with one hand and giving her mother a little hug. And her mother in return leaned toward him, placing a little kiss on his cheek, leaving a faint red mark.

They all were so happy. So very, very happy. Even Fluffy, woken from her nap by their singing, appeared to have a smile on her little furry face.

What a wonderful Thanksgiving this would be!

Not at all like *last* Thanksgiving.

Lydia stared out the car window.

Which seemed like a long, long time ago. . . .

"Hurry along, now," Lydia's mother, Brenda, said anxiously. "Make sure you have all of Fluffy's things."

Brenda, in a black parka with its hood pulled up, and Fluffy in her arms, stood by the front door of their Tudor home on Lake Minnetonka.

"Why can't we take her with us?" Lydia asked. She hated leaving the cat behind, even for a short while.

"You know Grandmother doesn't like cats."

Lydia, her arms laden with Fluffy's bed and food, moved past her mother, to the front door. "And a lot of other things," the little girl muttered.

Mother and daughter walked across the frozen front lawn toward the big brick Dutch colonial home next door. Behind them the lake—what Brenda could see of it—seemed forlorn, enveloped by a dense rolling fog. The dreary day fit her dreary mood.

Mrs. Jensen, a widow in her early seventies, whose husband had died the year before, answered their knock at her door. She was short and plump, in grey slacks and sweater, a pleasant expression on her fair Scandinavian face. Brenda thought Mrs. Jensen looked like a grandmother, even though the woman didn't have any grandchildren—or even children—of her own.

"Happy Thanksgiving, Mrs. Jensen," Brenda smiled.

"Come in, come in," the elderly woman greeted them.

Brenda and Lydia stepped inside the foyer. The house even smelled like a grandmother's house. Like chocolate chip cookies were baking in the oven. Not like booze and stale cigarettes.

"You're positive taking care of Fluffy won't be any trouble?" Brenda asked.

"Not at all," Mrs. Jensen assured her. "We get along just fine. I'm sure she'll feel at home in no time."

As if in response to that, Fluffy jumped from Brenda's arms to the floor and scampered down the long hall that led to the back of the house.

"She remembers where the kitchen is," Mrs. Jensen laughed.

"Here's Fluffy's things," Lydia said to the elderly woman, setting the items down on the floor. "Don't forget, she gets fed in the morning."

Mrs. Jensen smiled at the little girl. "I won't forget."

"I want to pay you something. . . ." Brenda dug in her coat pocket.

"Oh, no," Mrs. Jensen protested. "I won't hear of it."

"But I insist," Brenda replied firmly, and held out a

twenty dollar bill. "We'd have to pay to board her, you know. And this is so much better."

"Well. . . ." the older woman hesitated, looking at the money, which she then took and tucked it away in a pants pocket.

Brenda and Lydia were about to take leave of the woman when the little girl asked abruptly, "What happened to that lady that was here by the door?"

"You mean the statue?" Mrs. Jensen replied.

"Uh-huh."

"Oh, I got tired of her," Mrs. Jensen said lightly. "So I sold it."

That startled Brenda. "But . . . I thought it was an heirloom," she said amazed. She remembered Mrs. Jensen telling her about that exquisite bronze statue of a young Egyptian girl with arms outstretched holding a platter for salesmen to leaving their calling cards on, and how it had been in the office of the family's wholesale grocery store for generations.

"Well, now, my dear," Mrs. Jensen chided, "you can't afford to be sentimental at my age."

The word "afford" resonated in Brenda's head. Looking past Mrs. Jensen, she noticed that the grand hall tree with its beveled mirror and ornate dragon hooks was also gone. Had the woman gotten "tired" of that, too? Then something occurred to Brenda. Last week she saw the van of a real estate firm parked in front of Mrs. Jensen's house. Brenda didn't think much of it at the time, because that company often canvassed their neighborhood in search of leads to potential buyers.

"Mrs. Jensen," Brenda said, alarmed. "You're not selling the house?" It came out more a statement than a question.

175

The old woman's pleasant mask slipped, and her eyes turned moist, but her voice continued to be cheerful. "I'm looking for a smaller place, yes. Now that Gerald is gone, this house is really too big for me."

"But you've lived here so long," Brenda moaned. "And we'd miss you terribly." She fought back the tears that sprang to her eyes.

Lydia didn't bother holding back her tears. The little girl fell into the old woman's arms, sobbing uncontrollably.

Then Mrs. Jensen was crying, and Brenda buckled and joined them, and the three of them stood hugging each other in the foyer.

After a minute, Mrs. Jensen wiped her eyes with a tissue from the pocket of her slacks. "I'm not going very far away," she told them. "Maybe some place further north where it's not so expensive. We'll still see each other."

Brenda smiled bravely, for the benefit of Lydia and Mrs. Jensen, but inside she felt sick, like someone close to her had died. "Of *course,* we'll still see each other."

"You promise?" Lydia sniffed, looking at Mrs. Jensen.

"Promise," the old woman said, and stroked the little girl's head. Then she returned to her cheerfulness. "Now you must hurry along. There's a bad storm coming, and you have quite a drive up north. Oh . . . wait . . . there's something I want to give you. . . ."

The elderly woman left them and walked down the hall, disappearing into the kitchen. Then back she came with a white paper plate of chocolate chip cookies covered with clear wrap.

"Maybe these will pass the time in the car," she said handing the plate to Lydia. "I made them from scratch."

Mother and daughter thanked the woman and left, waving good-bye.

Trudging back across the lawn to their house, Lydia said glumly to her mother, "I wish we were spending Thanksgiving with Mrs. Jensen."

Brenda sighed. "I do, too, honey. I do, too."

The family was quiet on the three-hour trip north from Minnetonka to Brainard to visit Brenda's mother, who still lived in the same farmhouse Brenda grew up in. Brenda's father had died from a stroke seven years ago, when Lydia was only two. Her husband, Robert, had both of his parents living, but they resided in California, and the families rarely got together.

On the other side of St. Cloud, with heavy snow beginning to come down, Brenda said to her husband, "I wish there was something we could do to help Mrs. Jensen."

Robert, behind the wheel, nodded. "I do, too."

Earlier when they were packing the car (and Lydia was out of earshot), Brenda had told him of her fear that the elderly woman had run out of money.

"She should get a nice sum for the house," he had replied. But Brenda reminded him that the Jensens had had to mortgage their home some years ago when the grocery business ran into financial trouble. Now she was sure the woman was selling off her antique furniture, one piece at a time, just to make ends meet.

Brenda felt a familiar tightening in her neck, and one hand went there automatically to massage it, though she knew it would do no good.

"Migraine?" Robert asked, taking his eyes off the road, giving her a funny look, a combination of, "I'm sorry," and, "I knew this would happen."

Brenda dug in her purse and pulled out the prescription bottle of Sumatriptan tablets. She took one, washing it down with a swig of mineral water she'd brought along. Then she put the pills in the pocket of her cardigan sweater, in case she might need another.

"When will we get there?" Lydia asked from the back seat. The little girl had been quietly reading a book. She was casually dressed (like her parents) in jeans and a sweatshirt. Brenda didn't feel much like making them all dress up. Trips to see her mother were never very festive.

"Too soon," her husband said under his breath.

Brenda closed her eyes, resting her head against the car seat.

She hated her mother, a humorless, whiny vile witch of a woman. There was no other way to describe her. But what Brenda hated even more than the woman herself was the control she still had over Brenda after all these years. In seconds her mother could beat her down with a few choice words, just like when Brenda was a child.

"Robert, pull over!" Brenda cried.

He swerved the car off the two-lane highway onto the snowy shoulder.

Brenda flung open her car door, leaned out and threw up the Sumatriptan tablet. Her breakfast followed shortly, which she'd had over four hours ago. Her stomach, realizing long before she did that a migraine was coming, had shut itself down.

"Are you all right?" Robert asked softly.

Brenda nodded, involuntary tears sliding down her face. She reached for the bottle of mineral water, rinsed out her mouth and spit into the snow.

"Would you like a cookie, mommy?" Lydia asked sympathetically.

Brenda shook her head no.

"Let's turn around and go home," Robert suggested.

"We'll stop somewhere and call your mother and tell her you're sick."

"No!" Brenda said firmly. "I feel better. And we're almost there." She wasn't lying, she did feel better, and besides, she'd never hear the end of it if they missed Thanksgiving with her mother. They, after all, were bringing most of the food.

Robert sighed and steered the car back onto the road.

They were silent the rest of the way.

At the farmhouse, Brenda's mother didn't bother to come out on to the dilapidated front porch to greet them. Brenda could see her, scowling from the picture window, as they unloaded the car.

As she approached the farmhouse carrying the picnic basket of food, Robert behind her with a suitcase, Lydia bringing up the rear with her books, Brenda felt her stomach lurch again. She closed her eyes and took a deep breath, shutting out childhood memories that floated toward her out of the house like unwelcome ghosts.

She looked up at the old Victorian house and told herself that's all it was: a house, a structure of wood and stone. Nothing more.

She tried to open the wood door with its etched oval window but the door was locked; it had a special latch that automatically locked whenever the door shut. Robert had installed it for mother last summer after there were some area break-ins.

So, where was her mother? Brenda thought. She knocked on the door. She knew her mother had seen them. Just what kind of game was she playing, now? Then the door slowly opened and the smell of turkey greeted her, and suddenly Brenda was filled with hopefulness . . . perhaps this visit would be different.

But then there stood her mother, thin and bony, in a drab cotton dress (where was the new wool one she'd sent her?), a white shawl around her slumped shoulders, coarse grey hair pulled back in a bun, cigarette hanging from puckered lips.

"Where the hell have you been!" the old woman said crossly. "The turkey's been done for an hour. Now it's going to be tough as leather." Besides the nicotine, her mother's breath smelled of bourbon.

"I'm sorry, mother," Brenda said apologetically. "The traffic was heavy." Why did she have to lie? Why couldn't she just say that they'd gotten a late start, or that she was sick along the way? But then that would be Brenda's fault. And her mother already found enough fault with Brenda.

Her mother grunted. "You've put on some weight," she said.

"No," Brenda responded neutrally, "I don't think so. Maybe it's just this sweater."

"Well, you look fat."

Robert set the suitcase down. "It's so nice to see you, too," he said warmly to his mother-in-law. Which made Brenda smile. Robert's sarcasm always went right over the old woman's head.

"Hello, Grandmother," Lydia said, keeping her distance.

Her grandmother smiled—a rarity—showing tobacco-stained stumpy teeth, and reached out to her granddaughter, touching the little girl's head.

"Such pretty blonde hair," she said, then the smile dropped. "Too bad it'll most likely turn mousy, like your mother's."

"Thank you," Lydia said politely, having caught on to her father's way of handling the woman.

"Are you still writing those books?" Brenda's mother asked Robert, the word "those" coming out disdainfully. She

180

had turned abruptly away from her guests, heading for the rocking chair by the picture window.

"That's right," Robert responded, following the woman into the living room, settling into a rickety wicker chair, "I'm still writing suspense novels." He sighed and put some exasperation into his voice. "I wish I could do something more worthwhile, like work in a factory, but the darn things keep selling."

"I don't read trash," the grandmother said acerbically, putting her cigarette out in a blackened ashtray.

Robert nodded thoughtfully, "I remember . . . Your taste is more literary . . . tabloids, is it?"

Brenda smiled and took the picnic basket into the back kitchen. Lydia, wisely, had made herself scarce, having disappeared to an upstairs bedroom with her books.

The kitchen was small, with worn linoleum and appliances that had been new when television was young. Several times, Brenda and Robert had offered to give her mother a new kitchen, but the old woman declined, saying she liked things just the way they were. If so, she liked them dirty and dingy, Brenda thought.

She sighed and placed the picnic basket on a formica table. Sometimes, she envisioned the house empty, her mother gone. Oh, the things she would do *then!* How she would fix the house up! The front porch repaired, lace curtains in the living room windows, the fireplace roaring . . . all the things she'd never had when she lived here, all the things she had always wanted.

Hugging her arms to herself as if to keep warm, Brenda glanced toward the ceiling and shuddered. She could almost hear the house cry out. And something dawned on her: the house had been as much a victim as she.

"Someday," she whispered. "Someday."

There was a noise at the back door in the kitchen. A scratching sound. Brenda turned away from the table and walked over to the door. She looked out one of the grimy windowpanes. On the stoop was a yellow tom, shivering in the cold, snow swirling around it, one paw stretched out toward the door.

"Oh, my goodness," she said. "You poor thing."

She tried to open the back door but it was stuck. She gave it another good tug, but the door didn't budge. Probably hadn't been used for years, she thought. But then she noticed that the door had been nailed shut at the top . . . Her mother's idea of a back door lock. Brenda went through the kitchen to the living room, where Robert and her mother still sat, but silent now.

"Mother," she said, "there's a cat at the back door." She started to say, *Can it come in?* but she already knew the answer.

"Leave it be!" the old woman said sharply. "It's been hanging around here for a week and it can either freeze or scat!"

Upset, Brenda turned on her heels and went back to the kitchen. Maybe she could hide the cat in the basement overnight, then put it out in the morning after the storm had passed through. She peered through the back door window again, but the cat was gone, and she didn't see it anywhere.

"That witch," Brenda muttered as she went back to the table and began emptying the contents of the picnic basket each with an angry *klunk* onto the table: candied sweet potato casserole, cranberry sauce, dinner rolls, pumpkin pie.

The cranberry sauce was for her mother; no one else in the family liked it. She'd gotten the recipe from Mrs. Jensen, and went to a lot of trouble to make it.

182

SPICED CRANBERRIES

4 cups cranberries	5 allspice
5 cloves	2 sticks cinnamon
3 cups sugar	2 blades mace

Pick over and wash the berries. Place in a saucepan and cover with cold water. Tie spices in a cheesecloth bag and drop in with the berries. Cook until the berries burst. Remove spices, add sugar, and cook until the mixture is clear. Chill.

Just before serving add one bottle of Sumatriptan tablets.

And Brenda plucked the pills from the pocket of her cardigan, crushed them up with two spoons, and stirred the white drug into the red cranberry sauce.

At the table, as if in a dream, Brenda watched calmly as her mother dished the red cranberry sauce onto her plate next to slices of turkey (the meat, actually, was quite juicy, not tough at all).

Brenda knew what would happen if someone took too many pills; she'd read the paper that came with the tablets warning of an overdose: cardiac arrest.

Her mother took a big bite of the cranberry sauce and chewed. Brenda watched, as detached as the whipped cream sitting on the pumpkin pie.

Suddenly the old woman gagged and spat the food onto her plate, startling both Robert and Lydia.

"That tastes *terrible!*" her mother said, giving Brenda a mean look, wiping her mouth with the back of one hand.

"Must be the Sumatriptan," Brenda said sweetly.

"Well, next time use a different spice!" her mother snapped, and stabbed a piece of turkey with her fork.

"Yes, mother."

Brenda looked over at her daughter, who'd gone back to eating her food, unperturbed. But her husband—a fork-full of sweet potato casserole held frozen in the air—was anything *but;* his eyes were wide and frightened.

Robert lay awake in bed next to his wife in an upstairs room of the farmhouse. Outside, the howling snow-storm—which had hit around midnight—rattled the window-panes, shaking them with icy hands.

He looked over at his wife, who was sleeping deeply, though fitfully, her lovely face a twisted mask of subconscious pain.

It wasn't fair, he thought, that she should go through life tortured by her mother. Wasn't the physical abuse his wife endured as a child enough? The horror stories she'd told him, waking shivering from nightmares, were enough to fill a season of a daytime talk show. Did the abuse now have to turn psychological?

And what about him? As much as he loved Brenda—which was a lot—he had to admit he was growing weary of the effect that horrible woman was having on Brenda: moodiness, mi-graines, casting a pall on their lives that extended even to their bedroom. He tried to be supportive, understanding, but after all, he was only human.

He reached over with one hand, gently smoothing out the furrows on Brenda's brow. She moaned and turned her head away from him. No, it just wasn't fair. He wished that old witch was dead. A meaner person—man or woman—he had never encountered. Even the villains in his books weren't this vile.

Take the treatment of that poor kitty, for instance, the stray Brenda's mother wouldn't let her bring into the house. What the hell harm would that have done? And later, after supper, when Lydia tried to sneak a bowl of milk and a towel onto the ice-covered front porch for the pathetic little creature, the old biddy knocked the bowl from his daughter's hands, making the little girl cry, and chased the cat away with a broom. He could have *killed* that wretched old woman!

Which brought him around to what was really bothering him, what he'd been avoiding thinking about as he lay in bed: that Brenda really *had* tried to kill her mother.

At the table he knew Brenda hadn't been kidding about putting her migraine drug in the cranberry sauce—after all, his wife wasn't much of a kidder. And the look on Brenda's face! He couldn't quite describe it. He'd never seen it before—a kind of madness, like she'd lost her mind, and that really scared the hell out of him.

Later, after Brenda had gone to sleep, he had slipped out of bed and checked the pill bottle she'd left in the pocket of her sweater. It was empty, all right. Earlier, in the car, he had seen it full.

Robert put his hands behind his head and stared up at the cracked ceiling in the dark. No, he could never leave Brenda. He loved her too much. And he could never hurt his daughter, whom he loved even more. Where did that leave him?

Robert sat up in bed. But something had to be done, he thought, before Brenda got another chance to *really* harm her mother. . . .

He got out of bed and got into his robe, cinching the belt. God, it was cold in there! On woolen socks, he tiptoed out of the bedroom.

He could see light shining under the closed bedroom door across the hall where his mother-in-law slept. There were only two bedrooms upstairs. Their daughter was sleeping on the couch down in the living room. Good, he thought, the old woman was awake. Maybe they could have a nice heart-to-heart talk, with him being sincere for once.

Lightly he rapped on the door. No answer. Slowly he opened the bedroom door and peeked in.

The woman was asleep on the sagging bed, under the covers, snoring. Even in slumber her face had an unpleasant look. Folded across her rising stomach lay a supermarket tabloid, and in one limp hand dangled a cigarette, smoke spiraling lazily upward, just inches from the paper.

Robert was startled at what he saw. Didn't the crazy woman even know better than to smoke in bed? That smoldering cigarette could catch fire and . . . and. . . .

Just a minute, he thought, exhilarated, terrified. This was almost too perfect. All he had to do was back out of the room and wait. Wait until the paper caught fire, and then the blanket, and then the woman herself . . . .

But what if the whole house burned down?

What if it did? He'd seen the tormented look on his wife's face every time she approached the farmhouse, steeling herself to go in. Having the house gone would put an end to her tormented memories. And he'd have plenty of time to steer Brenda and Lydia safely to their car. Of course, it would be too late to help her mother. Tragically too late, that is.

He crept toward the bed.

Seized with excitement, heart racing . . . What if his plan took too long to happen? What if he went back to bed waiting for the inevitable and, damn, fell asleep? No, that was impossible; as excited as he felt, he could never fall asleep, and yet, still—perhaps he should help things along. . . .

With a finger he ever so gently scooted the corner of the tabloid to the butt of the smoldering cigarette.

With a crackle the tabloid ignited, then the tattered blanket beneath it, the flames dancing quickly . . . and the old woman woke up, eyes popping open like a vampire in its coffin. . . .

186

. . . and with him still standing there!

So he swatted at the flames on the blanket, with the old lady beneath it, and she yelped and started hitting him on the head.

"What the hell are you doing?" she snarled.

"I'm putting out the fire, what do you think?" he snarled back.

The fire was out. Smoke hung heavy in the air.

But instead of appreciation, the old woman pointed to the blackened bedspread and snapped, "Now see what you've done!"

Robert stared speechless at the tattered blanket that, even prior to the fire, had too many holes in it to count.

His mother-in-law threw back the bedspread, showing bony legs beneath a faded flannel nightgown, and slid out of bed. "Now I'll have to go get another."

Robert's face was burning, but his fire wouldn't be as easily put out—even if his spur-of-the-moment plan had been doused.

"You shouldn't smoke in bed," he said, wagging a finger at her.

"It's my house," she responded defiantly. "I'll do as I damn well please." She paused, then added, "And I *never* had any trouble before!"

He snorted in disgust, and turned, retreating to his room across the hall, where his wife slept unaware of the commotion, because of the squalling storm.

He was disgusted, all right. Disgusted with the stubborn old woman, and disgusted with himself . . . for even considering such a foolish plan . . . and for failing to carry it out.

From the yawning darkness of the upstairs, the grandmother descended to the living room, both her knees and the stairs creaking with every step. She had given her grand-daughter two blankets to sleep with on the couch, and she would take one back.

She thought about her son-in-law and frowned. Was she supposed to be *happy* that he had disturbed her sleep, which probably caused the paper to catch fire in the first place? She hadn't even finished reading the story about the clone of Son of Sam framing O.J.! Now she'd have to buy another *Galaxy Star*. Did he think they grew on trees? And what was he doing in her bedroom, anyway? Sick perverted creep . . . even that disappointment of a daughter of hers deserved better.

Not to mention that his thoughtless action of putting out the flames had ruined her favorite blanket. She *never* liked that man. He thought he was so superior. Once, she'd tried to read one of his books he sent her, but she ended up using it as a doorstop. It had too many characters to keep track of, and who did he think he was impressing, with all those big words. And the swearing! Christ Almighty. She wouldn't keep filth like that in the house.

Her frowned deepened into familiar grooves. She was quite aware that man made fun of her . . . but she never let on. He thought he was so smart. But not as smart as her!

The old woman smiled. Now Brenda, she wasn't smart at all. She could get that girl to jump through a hoop any old time she wanted.

The brief smile settled back into the frown. She had to admit, though, her daughter seemed almost defiant this trip. But the old woman would take care of that. In the morning she'd ask her to go to the cellar for something, then lock her down there for a minute or two (just like when her daughter was little, but only then it was a lot longer). That ought to bring back a nostalgic memory or two.

Lydia could use some discipline, too. That little girl was so spoiled and coddled, she didn't show the proper respect for her elders. But if the grandmother could have just a few days alone with the child, she could turn that around, all right . . . she'd have to finesse that, and soon.

She moved slowly toward her granddaughter through the chilly, shadowy living room. She liked the house that way: cold and dark and dreary. She wanted the happy little family to know, when they came for a visit, just what her life was like, just how hard she had it. Sometimes when they arrived, they'd look around for something they had sent—like a new dress or curtains. Try the trash, why don't you.

She didn't need *them* to tell *her* what it was that she needed, or how to live, neither.

She stood over the small figure of Lydia, curled up on the couch, covered up to her chin with the blankets. The girl was awake, her eyes big and round.

"What is it, Grandma?" she asked.

"Got to have one of those blankets."

"Grandma. . . ." the girl started to protest. But her grandmother had already pulled back the top cover, exposing the yellow tom curled up underneath.

"Why, you little. . . ." the old woman said through clenched teeth, not sure herself which insolent creature she was cursing at. Then she grabbed the cat by the scruff of its neck.

Lydia began to cry. "Please, Grandmother, it's so cold outside. I'll put it out in the morning."

"I'll put it out now!"

And the grandmother marched to the front door with the terrified cat, opened it and threw the animal out on the front porch into the blizzard.

189

"Now, *scat!*" she hollered.

But the cat didn't scat or even move, half-lying where it had landed.

"Won't go, will you?" the old woman said. She retreated a few steps to the fireplace and snatched up an old poker.

Her granddaughter, sobbing, ran past her—probably going to summon her parents, the old woman thought. But she didn't care. This was her house, and everyone had damn well better abide by her rules.

The old woman went out onto the porch, into the storm, and threw the poker at the cat, missing her target by a mere inch, the steal rod flying over the animal's head, disappearing into the drifting snow.

The cat screeched and fled—but not out into the yard. The animal ran past the woman back into the house.

And the wind blew, slamming the front door shut, locking the old woman out.

She banged at the front door, but no one saw her. She screamed, but no one heard her. She sank to her knees in the cold, cold snow, fingernails scratching at the front door . . . but no one came to rescue her.

And no one was there to provide her a blanket, except the snow.

The Ford Thunderbird turned off the two-lane highway and down a winding lane lined with pine trees, their snow-covered boughs shimmering in the late-morning sun.

Lydia leaned forward anxiously in the back seat, peering through the front windshield.

Would they ever get there? she wondered.

Then around the next bend in the lane, there was the farmhouse—just like in the card—but even prettier with a fresh coat of white paint, the railing on the grand porch repaired, and new lace curtains hanging in the windows.

Lydia's father parked the car in front of the house, next to a trio of birch trees.

"I'll get the suitcases," he said. "Mother, you take in the picnic basket, and Lydia, you're in charge of the cat."

But when he opened the car door, Fluffy leapt from the backseat, over the front, and scampered out before Lydia could even move.

"Fluffy!" Lydia called, afraid that the cat might run away because she'd never been there before. But the feline headed toward the front door of the farmhouse; she knew where she was going.

Then out of the screen door came a plump old woman, in an apron covering a navy dress, her arms outstretched, a look of joy on her grandmotherly face. Staying close by her feet was the yellow tom.

"Hello, Mrs. Jensen," Lydia's father said, coming up the front porch steps, a suitcase in each hand.

"Now . . . " the woman scolded, "I thought we all agreed to call me 'Grandmother'."

He smiled and put the suitcases down and gave the woman a hug. "Hello, Grandmother," he smiled.

"Happy Thanksgiving, Grandmother," said Lydia's mother. "It's so nice to see you."

"Grandmother!" called Lydia, and bounded up the steps and into the woman's arms. She smelled of roasted turkey, her bosom soft and warm.

"Come, let's all go inside," Grandmother said. "We'll have some hot punch in the living room before dinner is served. I've gotten the fireplace working, you know."

"How wonderful," Lydia's mother exclaimed. "The house looks so beautiful, just like I imagined it could."

Lydia started to follow the group inside, but remembered

the card she'd left in the backseat of the car.

She turned and hurried back to the Ford, her patent leather shoes crunching on the snow, and retrieved the card. As the little girl stood next to the car, she looked toward the farmhouse. Through the big front picture window she could see the crackling fire in the living room fireplace, and her parents laughing as Grandmother served them punch off the big bronze tray of the Egyptian lady.

Her mother had bought all the things back.

And a smile appeared on Lydia's pretty pink lips.

She wasn't at all sorry about what happened last Thanksgiving. About the front door blowing shut, locking her real grandmother out. Nor was she sorry the wind stung the old woman's toes and bit her nose (and worse). Or was she even sorry she ignored the old woman's cries (staying huddled on the living room steps) which blended with the storm before growing faint, then silent.

Because *that* grandmother wasn't the kind of grandmother a grandmother *should* have been!

The little girl skipped toward the house, card in hand, singing as she went, "Spring over the ground, like a hunting-hound, for this is Thanksgiving Day!"

Too Many Tomcats

It was a little after 10 p.m. when Ernie and Marie Finley climbed the steps of their modest white stucco house, after a Saturday evening out. Ernie was a small man, about five foot five, with a mustache and thinning brown hair; he had his key chain in his hands, searching for the right one in the dark. Marie, who was twenty pounds heavier than her husband, her dyed-black hair piled on top of her head adding to her five foot ten frame, stood next to him on the porch, biting her lower lip to keep from snapping "Can't you hurry up!" That would have spoiled a perfect evening.

They had gone to a new French restaurant, Le Perroquet, and not once during the leisurely meal had Marie thought of their little Sarah, left at home with a babysitter. Later, they went to a movie—a comedy—where she was comfortably distracted during the feature. But as soon as the end credits began to roll, anxiety began to roll over her, and she couldn't wait to get out of the theater and get home. She suddenly felt heartsick being away from Sarah.

When Ernie suggested they stop for ice cream, Marie had said quickly, "No. I'm trying to lose weight." (Never mind the four-course dinner topped off with cherries flambé.) Her husband just smiled; she knew he understood. That's what she loved most about him.

Ernie finally got the key in the lock and opened the front door and they both stepped inside.

Everything in the living room was purple—or shades of

purple, from lavender to dusty rose. Ernie had gotten the idea several years ago when the middle-aged couple was trying to conceive. He'd read somewhere that the color purple sparked passion, and so he set about redecorating the house. It wasn't easy finding a purple couch.

The television—the only furnishing in the front room that wasn't purple—was on, volume low. Across from the TV, on the purple couch, sat the babysitter, a neighborhood girl named Misty. She was a pretty, pretty plump teen-ager, with flawless, cream-colored skin and short blonde hair cut like the Dutch Boy on the paint can. She looked up from a magazine as Ernie and Marie entered.

"Is Sarah asleep?" Marie asked in a whisper.

The babysitter nodded.

Marie sat down next to her on the couch. "Tell me about your evening."

Misty sighed; this was not her first visit to the Finleys. "Well," she said, "first off, right after you left, she started lookin' for you. Going from room to room, crying. . . ."

Marie looked sharply at Ernie, who stood next to the couch. "I *knew* we shouldn't have gone out," she told him. She turned back to the sitter. "Then what?" she asked.

"Then I played the tape of cartoons you rented, and she sat on my lap and watched for a while . . . she seemed to like the ones about Garfield, best . . . but then she got bored and started lookin' for you again."

"Did you give her the cookies I left on the counter?" Marie asked.

"She wouldn't eat them. But she did drink the milk. I warmed it up like you showed me. After that, I put her to bed and shut the door and she cried herself to sleep."

Marie sat silently, her hands clasped tightly in her lap, feeling like a terrible parent.

Misty stood. "Well, if that's all, I better go. See you next Saturday night?"

Marie looked up anxiously at Ernie, who was getting money out of his wallet to pay the girl.

"No," he said softly, looking back at Marie. "We won't be needing you." He handed Misty the money. "I'll drive you home."

After they left, Marie tiptoed down the lavender carpeted hallway to Sarah's room. The door was shut and she quietly turned the knob and slowly opened the door.

Moonlight poured in through a window and fell across the tiny bed in the center of the room where Sarah lay sleeping, her pink tummy gently rising and falling. Marie smiled, filled with love and joy, as she moved toward the little form.

Sarah must have heard Marie because she woke and jumped from the bed into Marie's arms. Marie fell to her knees, hugging the kitten tightly to her chest, kissing the animal—all about its furry white face.

"Mommy's home," she purred. "Mommy's home."

The little kitten purred back.

"Now go to sleep," she said, and returned the kitten to the bed, which was really a doll's bed.

They had gotten the pink, plastic bed—which came with a little matching dresser and night stand—shortly after bringing the kitten home from the Humane Society. Ernie spotted the doll set in the window of Ingram's Department store, and bought it as a joke. But Marie immediately cleared out the extra bedroom and put the little furniture in. At first, she placed the tiny dresser over against one wall, the bed against the other wall, and the nightstand by the window. But that looked silly. So she moved everything to the center of the room, where it was now. Recently, she added a poster of Garfield to the wall and one of a kitten hanging by its front paws from a limb, with the words: Hang In There.

Marie quietly left Sarah's room, closing the door gently, and walked down the hallway to the kitchen, where she found Ernie siting at the round oak table. He had a serious expression on his face. She suspected he was upset with her for canceling the babysitter.

Marie pulled out a chair and sat next to him.

"I'm sorry about our Saturday night dates," she began, "but I'm just a wreck whenever I have to leave Sarah."

"I know," he said.

"We'll be able to go out again soon," Marie promised, "when she's a little bit older."

"That's fine."

Ernie's face remained somber, so Marie leaned toward her husband and asked, "Then . . . what's wrong?"

"It's time to have her spayed, Marie," he said.

Marie pulled back, horrified. "Oh, no. Not that."

"Now, Marie," Ernie said sternly, as if he were talking to a child, "we discussed this before we got Sarah, and you agreed."

"I know," she said, desperation building in her voice, "but I *hate* the idea. It's so . . . so *inhumane*. Can't we just keep her inside the house all the time?"

Ernie shook his head. "You know she'll get out . . . it happened last week . . . and there are just too many tomcats in the neighborhood to risk that."

Marie felt tears welling in her eyes. "I don't want anybody cutting her open . . . She's too little to have that done. It's not the right time. We'll spay her later, I promise."

"It *is* the right time," Ernie argued. "She's four and a half months old and that's when the vet said to bring her in. The longer we wait, the harder it will be on Sarah."

Marie sat expressionless, but the rage was building up

within her like lava in a volcano.

"I've already scheduled an appointment for Monday with Dr. Harden," Ernie continued. "He was very gentle with Sarah when we took her to him from the Humane Society. You said so yourself."

Marie said nothing.

"He'll be very careful."

And now Marie exploded. "How would *you* like being neutered? How would you like never being able to have children?"

Ernie's face fell; there was hurt in his eyes.

"I'm sorry," Marie said softly. "I didn't mean it like that. It's not entirely your fault we don't have our 2.5 quota."

Ernie took one of her hands in his and spoke earnestly. "Marie, if we don't have her spayed, and one of the toms gets her, and she has kittens, would you be able to give the babies away? I don't think so. Nor would I. And this house is too small for a lot of cats—even 2.5—that would have even more kittens we wouldn't have the heart to give away."

Marie was silent for a few moments, then she sighed. "All right, Ernie, we'll have her spayed. But I don't like it one bit. Not one little bit."

Dr. Tom Harden, dark-haired, thirty-five years old, his blue eyes setting off well-chiseled features, washed his hands at the stainless steel sink in the operating room of his veterinarian hospital.

In the center of the room, on a shiny chrome table, lay the Finley's kitten, stretched out on its back, still under the anesthesia, its belly yellow from the iodine he had just spread on the closed incisions.

The operation had gone well, but then, why shouldn't it? He was, after all, one of the best damn vets in the whole state, if not the whole United States—even if the rest of the country was denied his expertise because he was stuck in a backwater town in the middle of nowhere.

A backwater town, however, did have its advantages. Like low cost of living, inexpensive housing, no traffic jams, short lines at the bank . . . And a bevy of lovely, lonely women. Juicy tomatoes just ripe for the pickin' and a very low incidence of sexually transmitted disease. He'd sampled plenty of the local harvest in this sleepy river town.

It didn't matter that he was married. With children. It was the hunter/gatherer's inalienable right to cat from bush to bush to satisfy his hunger. Of course, his wife didn't see it that way. So after the first time she caught him, he'd been careful ever since. Dr. Harden picked up the kitten and took it over to one of the cages and placed the slumbering animal inside, in the doll's bed the Finleys had brought along.

Was that couple *weird!* Really sick in the head, clinically, certifiable. Treating the kitten, which they called Sarah, like it was their child. He'd met some pretty neurotic people in his line of work, but they took the cake.

Furthermore, much to his annoyance, the Finleys had insisted on staying and keeping vigil in the reception area until the operation was over. Now he would have to go out and talk to them, as if he didn't have enough to do.

He left the operating room and went through a connecting door to the front of the building, which was half-office, half-reception area; the two being separated by a high counter. As he passed through the office, the receptionist, Heather—a pretty young thing just out of high school—looked up from her typewriter and gave him a coy smile.

My God, she was luscious. With her long slender legs, curvaceous body, and wild blond hair, Heather was a Barbie doll come to life . . . Too bad their relationship had to come to an end. This was one tomato that would need to die on the vine.

He entered the reception area, with its brown paneled walls, red vinyl chairs, and green tiled floor, which Mr. Finley was pacing like an expectant father; the man reminded Dr. Harden of somebody . . . who? Ah! Mr. Whipple from the old toilet-paper commercials!

Mrs. Finley, who must have been half again her husband's size—and could probably hurt her husband if she wanted to—sat with her hands clenched tightly in her lap, worry lines etched across her forehead. The woman's hair, piled on her head in huge looping curls as if wrapped around soup cans, looked purple under the fluorescent ceiling lights.

Harden put on his kindly doctor face as he approached the couple.

The moment Mrs. Finley spotted him she jumped up from her chair and rushed toward him.

"Oh, doctor," she said anxiously, "how is Sarah?"

"She's just fine," he told her with a smile.

Mr. Finley, joining his wife, asked, "Can we see her now?"

"I don't think that would be wise. She's resting."

"Oh, please," the woman said, pitifully. "Can't we see her for just a minute?"

"No," Dr. Harden said firmly. "I don't want her disturbed." Then patronizingly he added, "Why don't you folks run along home. You can see her in the morning."

Mr. Finley nodded, uncertainly, and turned to go, but the missus stood her ground. "Why can't we take Sarah with us?" the stupid woman asked. "The operation's over."

"Because you can't," Harden snapped, making Mrs. Finley frown, so he quickly explained, "We need to keep her overnight, for observation."

Which was ridiculous. No one checked on the animals

during the night, the beasts were on their own; but Mrs. Finley seemed to accept these conventional words, and it was the clinic's policy to keep pets overnight after even a simple operation, mostly to justify higher charges.

Dr. Harden watched the pair go out the front door. The whole conversation had been ridiculous, he thought. In fact, going through with the operation at all had been ridiculous. Because in the morning the cat would be dead.

As he walked back into the office area, Heather rose from her desk and came to him, putting her arms around his waist, looking up into his face, with open, inviting lips.

"Did you tell her yet?" she asked.

"Who?"

"Who do you think?"

"No. I'm waiting for the right time."

Heather drew back, patted her tummy with one hand, and said, "Well you'd better tell her soon because I'm beginning to show. And I want a last name for our child *before* it's born."

He gave her a half-hearted smile. "I'll tell her this weekend."

Heather smiled back, her arms around him again. "I know you will, so I won't have to." Then she said cheerfully, "Oh, by the way, my father said he'll put in the new water heater on Sunday. I told him to use the key under the mat to let himself in."

Dr. Harden nodded numbly.

"Excuse me." A voice said.

Harden quickly pushed the girl away, and turned to see Mrs. Finley standing at the counter. She had something in her hands.

"The pillow fell out of the bed in the car," the woman said as she held out a little square white piece of fluff. "Would you please see that Sarah gets it?"

"Yes," Dr. Harden said tersely, his face red with both embarrassment and rage. "Just leave it on the counter."

Mrs. Finley nodded and thanked him and left. This time for good, he hoped.

Heather returned to his side. "I don't think she heard us," the girl said quietly.

He gave her a disgusted look, but Heather just shrugged. "And even if she did, it doesn't matter; people get married and divorced all the time." And she returned to her work at the desk.

Harden, feeling sick to his stomach, left the office area and went down a short hall to his private office, stepping over a bucket filled with rainwater from a recent downpour. He entered the room and shut the door, then slumped down in the leather chair behind his desk.

The building needed a new roof and a sprinkler system to bring it up to code. Then there was the foundation that cracked. And equipment that should be replaced.

But he didn't have enough money for all that.

He did, however, have insurance. Insurance that would give him a brand new building and state-of-the-art equipment . . . if ever there were a disaster.

He'd been planning it for weeks, for just the right time. Which seemed like tonight because he didn't want many animals to die—his mission in life was to attend to the needs of God's creatures, after all—and there was only one animal being boarded in the building.

The Finleys would just have to get themselves another "baby." And it would serve those lunatics right, treating a cat better than a person.

He supposed he could have let the couple take their pet home with them, but that break from standard operating procedure might have tipped Heather. Lately she must have sensed his coolness, and everything needed to seem normal. And if no animals were present during the accident, that might raise suspicion. That's why he went ahead with the kitten's operation.

His original plan, which spread through his brain like the seeping gas of the faulty water heater, had been to destroy only the building. But recently, since he found out he was to be a father again, the plan took on an added element: Heather. He'd read somewhere about an incident, a freakish accident, where leaking gas from a water heater filled a room, and the simple act of flipping on a nearby light switch was enough to spark an explosion that had blown up the house.

He'd return late tonight, and put out the pilot light and open the gas line, and let the back room fill with propane fumes.

At eight in the morning, Heather would enter the back room to feed the animals as she always did, turn on the lights and KA-BOOM! creatures great and small would wing their way to heaven.

He smiled, leaning back in his office chair, hands hooked behind his head, elbows fanned out.

After all, why not kill two "burdens" with one stone?

Marie Finley couldn't sleep. She lay in bed and heard the hall clock strike one, then two. Next to her, Ernie was gently snoring.

How could he sleep so peacefully, she thought, *when their baby lay in a cold, dark cage?*

Quietly she slipped out of bed and wandered down the hall to Sarah's room, where the door stood open. She looked in.

Moonlight shown in past the curtains casting long shadows from the branches of a magnolia tree across the small, forlorn-looking doll furniture in the center of the room, particularly without Sarah's little bed. Marie felt tears spring to her eyes; she missed Sarah so much. She entered the room and sat down on the lavender carpeted floor, taking the place of the bed.

She thought about Dr. Harden. She didn't like that man very much. Maybe Ernie hadn't noticed, but the doctor talked down to them, like they were just children to be dealt with; even though his mouth smiled, there was contempt in his eyes.

And there was another thing she didn't like about the vet: he was a womanizer. She'd overheard the conversation between him and his pregnant secretary when she went back to deliver the pillow.

Marie, still seated on the floor in her pajamas, folded her hands and sighed. The bad rumors about the doctor she'd heard in the locker room after her water aerobics class must be true.

His poor wife—Jenny was her name. She was an attractive woman, so why would he want to stray? Marie couldn't understand it. She'd seen Jenny recently at the grocery store, looking sad and weary, with her two small, well-behaved children, in tow.

Her thoughts turned back to Sarah. She doubted very much if Dr. Harden—or his pregnant girlfriend—would be checking on Sarah during the night, who had probably woken up from the anesthesia by now, scared, wondering why she was stuck in a cage, wondering what she had done to deserve being put there, mewing and mewing for her mother and father. . . .

Marie sat up straighter as an awful thought crossed her mind. What if something had gone wrong during the operation? What if there had been complications caused by the doctor's malpractice, and he was hiding it from them?

What if Sarah weren't even *alive?* What if she'd died during the operation and that devious doctor didn't want to tell them? Why else wouldn't he let them see her?

Marie stood up, caught in the clutches of terror, which was squeezing the very breath out of her. Maybe *that* explained the sense of foreboding she'd had on the ride home from the animal clinic, and why she couldn't now get to sleep.

Marie bolted from the room and went quickly back down the hall to her bedroom. She'd made up her mind. She was going out to that animal hospital right now! She didn't care if it was the middle of the night. Hadn't the secretary said there was a key under the doormat?

Quietly, she slipped out of her nightgown and into a cotton housedress. Across the room, Ernie slept soundly, his chest rising and falling.

She wouldn't wake him to discuss the matter; he would only try to dissuade her. Besides, everyone knows that a mother knows best.

A three-quarter moon hung high in the sky, illuminating the way through the backcountry road. Soon, Marie pulled her car into the gravel parking lot of the animal hospital, and got out, quietly shutting the car door. The building was dark and silent. The only noise was the rustling of the leaves in the trees from a cool summer night breeze.

She found the key under the rubber front door mat and let herself in.

The place smelled funny. But then, animal hospitals always did. She didn't know how anyone could stand to work in one. But after a moment the bad smell went away, or anyway she got used to it.

Then cautiously she moved through the dark reception

room and into the office area and down the hallway to the back, where the animals were kept.

She opened the door and stood there a minute, feeling a little dizzy. It was hard to see in the dark. Marie's hand moved to the nearby light switch. Her fingers were on it, ready to flick the switch, when she suddenly pulled her hand back. The lights might attract someone's attention. And she didn't want that. She could be caught for breaking and entering, though she didn't at all see it that way.

With her eyes now accustomed to the dark, she moved ahead toward the cages, where her feet bumped into a metal bucket, tipping it over, water spilling onto the cement floor making an awful clatter. She froze.

Then from one of the cages came a pitiful sound, tiny and frightened, and Marie ran toward it, recognizing the cry of her baby. She quickly unlatched the cage door and reached in and withdrew Sarah and held the animal to her chest.

"You're alive . . . You're alive," Marie sobbed with joy.

But the kitten felt limp in her hands, and Marie's joy was replaced with fear as she realized that Sarah was really sick. And suddenly Marie felt sick, too, stomach nauseous, head pounding.

"Let's get out of here," she told the kitten, and she snatched the little bed out of the cage and ran from the room, shutting the door behind them.

In the outer office she scribbled a note on a piece of typing paper, leaving it on the desk, and that's when she saw the little pillow, still left on the counter. Harden hadn't even bothered to give it to Sarah. That thoughtless bastard.

She left the building, locking the front door, returning the key to its place under the mat. In the car, on the way home, she glanced anxiously at Sarah who rested in the bed, her head on the pillow. The kitten seemed to be doing better, even giving Marie a mew or two.

Marie felt better, too, breathing the fresh country air coming in the car window. The nausea and dizziness were gone, but replaced by indignation and fury. They were never, ever going to go back there!

Dr. Harden had never slept so good, knowing that in the morning all his troubles would be gone. He was especially cheerful at the breakfast table, where his pretty wife, Jenny, served him pancakes and sausage. He must have been too cheerful, though, because she gave him a suspicious look. So he launched into a tirade about that stupid, lazy secretary of his whom he'd like to replace. Jenny, cutting the link sausage with a knife, gave him another funny look that he couldn't quite interpret. He promised himself that if all went as planned he would stay faithful to his wife.

For a while, anyway.

As he ate his breakfast, he thought the fire department or police might call, telling him that his building had blown up, but the phone didn't ring. He looked at his watch. It was a little too soon, really. Heather didn't show up for work until eight. Then it would be another few minutes before she went into the back to feed the Finley's cat.

He stalled around until eight, then left the house and got into his car for the ten-minute drive.

He took his time along the winding country road, the morning overcast and cool, eyes fixed on the horizon, looking for signs of destruction.

Then around the bend, the animal hospital came into view, still standing. He slammed on his brakes, coming to a halt the middle of the road, not knowing what to do.

Had Heather not shown up for work? No, her car was parked in the lot. He needed to wait a few more minutes. But where? Not in the middle of the road. And if he retreated, some other car coming along might see him, and blow a hole in his story.

He decided to forge ahead and play the hero who arrived just as the building exploded. The hero who tried in vain to save his secretary and the lone animal inside, but was driven back by the heat and flames. He smiled, liking that idea.

He parked his car at the far end of the lot and sat and waited, feeling safe inside. But at eight-thirty, when nothing had happened, he disgustedly threw open the car door and got out and stomped toward the front door.

Inside, he found Heather at her desk, hanging up the phone.

"There you are," she said. "I just called the gas company . . . I think there's some sort of leak, so I opened the windows."

"You opened the windows?!" he repeated, realizing his plan had just dissipated with the gas.

"Well, yes," she replied. "Do you want the place to blow up? You look terrible . . . Is anything the matter?"

"No," he snapped, then asked, "Why didn't you go in the back to feed the cat?"

"Because I didn't *have* to," she said irritably. "Mrs. Finley came and got it in the middle of the night." She waved a piece of paper in his face. "She left me a note . . . Say, what's wrong with you?"

He didn't answer, but stomped down the hallway to the back.

He opened the door to the darkened room where the metal cages sat, all empty. The back door was ajar, held open with a tin bucket.

Goddamnit! he thought. *The bitch let all the gas out.*

And he flicked on the lights.

He was wrong.

Ernie Finley relaxed in his overstuffed lavender recliner as he read the evening newspaper. Marie, curled up on the purple couch across from him, was working on a needlepoint sampler of a cat, while Sarah frolicked on the carpet between them, batting about a little rose-colored pouch that contained catnip.

"Unbelievable," Ernie said, shaking his head, folding the paper and putting it down.

"What's that, dear?" Marie asked, her eyes still glued to the sampler.

"The accident at the veterinarian hospital," he answered.

"Oh, yes," she said, working the needle in the material. "I guess it destroyed the back half of the building."

Marie looked up from the sampler, and their eyes met. Ernie, feeling a lump in his throat, got out of his chair and sat next to her on the couch, taking one of her hands in his.

"Thank God you drove out there last night and saved our little girl," he said, his voice cracking with emotion.

Marie set the sampler aside. Patted his hand with hers. "Yes. I'm glad I listened to my inner voice."

"And if you hadn't left that note," Ernie went on, "the receptionist would have gotten hurt, instead of the doctor." He paused and shook his head. "I feel so sorry for him."

"I don't," Marie said archly.

Ernie looked at his wife, surprised by her coldness. "Marie, how can you say such a thing? The blast blew off his . . ." Ernie swallowed, unable to say the word. "He'll never be able to have more children."

"Well, he's already had his quota," she explained, and told him about the pregnant receptionist.

And he told her about a few others he'd heard about at the barbershop.

"So you see," Marie said, sticking the needle in the sampler, pulling the thread through, "everything's turned out for the good."

"I guess you're right, my dear," Ernie admitted. "You always are." He gave her a small peck of a kiss. "Anyway, there's one less tomcat in the neighborhood."